Bond, Michael

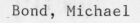

Paddington helps out

WP-PB-88

DATE DUE

Paddington Helps Out

By

MICHAEL BOND

Illustrated by Peggy Fortnum

A YEARLING BOOK

Published by
DELL PUBLISHING CO., INC.
1 Dag Hammarskjold Plaza
New York, N.Y. 10017
Copyright © 1960 by Michael Bond
ISBN: 0-440-46802-7

Reprinted by arrangement with
Houghton Mifflin Company
Printed in the United States of America
Twenty-sixth Dell printing—July 1985

CW

CONTENTS

CHAPTER ONE

A Picnic on the River

PADDINGTON sat up in bed with a puzzled expression on his face. Happenings at number thirty-two Windsor Gardens, particularly breakfast, always followed a strict time-table and it was most unusual for anything to waken him quite so early.

He took a careful look around his room, but everything seemed to be in its place.

The photograph of his Aunt Lucy, taken shortly before she entered the home for retired bears in Lima, was on the table beside the bed, along with

7

his jar of special marmalade and several other items.

His old hat and duffle coat were both hanging on the door peg, and his Peruvian centavos were under the pillow.

Most important of all, when he lifted the bedclothes and peered underneath, his small leather suitcase with its secret compartment containing his scrap-book and a number of important papers was still at the bottom of the bed.

Paddington heaved a sigh of relief. Although he had lived with the Browns for over a year he had never quite got used to having a room of his own and he wasn't the sort of bear who believed in taking chances.

It was at that point, just as he was absent-mindedly dipping his paw into the marmalade jar before going back to sleep, that Paddington pricked up his ears and listened.

There were voices—quite a number of voices— coming from the garden. Several times he heard a door bang, and then, in the distance, he heard a noise remarkably like that of chinking plates followed by the sound of Mr. Brown shouting orders.

Paddington scrambled out of bed and hurried across the room to the window. It sounded most interesting and he didn't like to think he might be missing anything. As he peered through the glass he nearly fell over backwards with astonishment at the sight which met his eyes. He breathed heavily on the window-pane and rubbed it with his paw to make sure he wasn't dreaming the whole thing.

For there, on the lawn outside, all the Brown family—Mr. and Mrs. Brown and Jonathan and Judy—were gathered round a large wicker basket. Not only that, but as he watched, Mrs. Bird, their housekeeper, came out of the kitchen carrying a huge plate piled high with sandwiches.

Paddington climbed off the window-sill and hurried downstairs. It was all very mysterious and it definitely needed investigating.

" Trust Paddington! " said everyone as he came through the kitchen door just as they were shutting the lid of the hamper.

" That bear can smell out a marmalade sandwich a mile away," grumbled Mrs. Bird.

" Honestly," said Judy, waving her finger at him. " It was meant to be a surprise. We got up specially early."

Paddington looked from one to the other with growing surprise.

" It's all right, Paddington," laughed Mrs. Brown. " There's no need to be alarmed. We're only going for a picnic on the river."

" And we're having a competition," cried Jonathan, waving a fishing net in the air. " Dad's promised a prize to whoever makes the first catch."

Paddington's eyes grew rounder and rounder. "A picnic?" he exclaimed. "I don't think I've ever been for a picnic on the river before."

"That's good," said Mr. Brown, twirling his moustache briskly. "Because you're going on one now. So hurry up and eat your breakfast. It's a lovely day and we may as well make the most of it."

Paddington needed no second bidding and while the Browns were busy packing the rest of the picnic gear into the car he hurried back indoors where his breakfast was waiting. He liked doing new things and he was looking forward to the day's outing. One of the nicest things about living with the Browns was the number of surprises he had.

"I hope I've never ever done everything, Mrs. Bird," he said as she came into the dining-room to see if he'd finished his toast and marmalade. "I shouldn't have any surprises left then!"

"Hmm," replied Mrs. Bird sternly, as she bundled him out of the room. "You'll be getting a surprise if you don't wash those bacon-and-egg stains off your whiskers before we go out. I've never known such a bear for getting in a mess."

Paddington put on his injured expression as he disappeared into the hall. "I was only trying to be quick, Mrs. Bird," he explained.

Nevertheless, he hurried upstairs to the bathroom. There were several important things to be done before he went out for the day. First of all there was his suitcase to be packed, and then he had to consult his atlas. Paddington was very keen on geography and he was interested in the thought of having a picnic on the river. It sounded most unusual.

" I don't know why it is," said Mrs. Bird, as she adjusted her hat for what seemed like the fortieth time, " but whenever this family goes anywhere it always takes enough to keep a regiment for a month."

The Browns were packed into the car jogging along the road towards the river. Besides the Browns, Mrs. Bird and Paddington, there was the hamper, a gramophone, a pile of records, a number of parcels and some fishing nets—not to mention several sunshades, a tent and a pile of cushions.

Mrs. Brown shifted uncomfortably as she agreed with Mrs. Bird. Paddington's leather suitcase was sticking in her back and his old hat, which he insisted on wearing in case of sunstroke, kept tickling the side of her face.

" Is it much farther? " she asked.

Paddington, who was sitting beside her on the front seat, consulted his map. " I think it's the next turning on the right," he announced, following the route with his paw.

" I do hope so," said Mrs. Brown. They had already taken one wrong turning that morning when

Paddington had followed a piece of dried marmalade peel on his map by mistake.

"Fancy turning right at a piece of dried marmalade peel," grumbled Mr. Brown. "That policeman didn't like it at all."

Anxious to make amends, Paddington stuck his head out of the window and sniffed.

"I think we must be getting near, Mr. Brown," he called. "I can smell something unusual."

"That's the gas works," said Mr. Brown, following the direction of Paddington's paw. "The river's on *this* side."

Just as he spoke they swept round a corner and there, straight in front of them, was a broad expanse of water.

Paddington's eyes lit up as they all clambered out of the car and while the others were unloading the supplies he stood on the water's edge and surveyed the scene. He was most impressed.

The towpath was crowded with people and there were boats everywhere. Rowing boats, canoes, punts and sailing boats with their white sails billowing in the wind. As he watched, a steamer packed with more people swept by, sending a large wave shooting across the water and causing all the smaller boats to rock. Everyone on board seemed very gay and happy and several of them pointed towards Paddington and waved.

Paddington raised his hat in reply and then turned to the others. "I think I'm going to like the river," he announced.

"I do hope so, dear," said Mrs. Brown uneasily. "It *is* your treat."

She looked at the row of boats moored by the landing stage. The day before it had seemed a very good idea of Mr. Brown's to have a picnic on the river. But now they were actually here she had a nasty feeling in the back of her mind and she knew Mrs. Bird was feeling the same way. Close to, the boats looked awfully small.

"Are you sure they're safe, Henry?" she asked, looking at them nervously.

"Safe?" echoed Mr. Brown, as he led the way on to the landing stage. "Of course they're safe, Mary. You just leave everything to me."

"I'll put you in charge of all the ropes and things, Paddington," he called. "That means you can steer."

"Thank you very much, Mr. Brown," said Paddington, feeling most important. His eyes gleamed with excitement as he climbed into the boat and carefully examined everything with his paws.

"The boatman's rather busy," said Mr. Brown, as he helped the others in. "So I said we would shove off by ourselves."

" Paddington! " exclaimed Mrs. Brown, as she picked Mrs. Bird's best sun hat off the floor of the boat. " *Do* mind what you're doing with that fishing net. You'll have someone's head off."

" I'm sorry, Mrs. Bird," said Paddington. " I was only testing it."

" All right," said Mr. Brown, as he settled himself on his seat and took a firm grip on the oars. " Here we go. Stand by at the helm, Paddington."

" Do *what*, Mr. Brown? " cried Paddington.

" Pull on the ropes," shouted Mr. Brown. " Come on—left paw down."

" Oh, dear," said Mrs. Bird nervously, as she clutched the side of the boat with one hand and gripped her sunshade with the other. Out of the corner of her eye she could already see a number of people staring in their direction.

In the back of the boat Paddington pulled hard on the two ropes tied to the rudder. He wasn't quite sure whether Mr. Brown had meant *his*, Mr. Brown's left, or his own left, so he pulled both just to make certain. Everyone waited expectantly while Mr. Brown strained on the oars.

" I should have thought, Henry," said Mrs. Brown, after a few moments had gone by, " it would have been much easier if you'd untied the boat from the landing stage first."

14

" What! " exclaimed Mr. Brown. He mopped his brow and looked crossly over his shoulder. " Hasn't anyone done that yet? "

" I'll do it, Mr. Brown," called Paddington importantly, as he clambered along the side of the boat. " I'm in charge of ropes."

The Browns waited patiently while Paddington examined the rope. He wasn't very good at knots because they were rather difficult with paws, but eventually he announced that all was ready.

" Right! " shouted Mr. Brown, as he braced himself once more. " Here we go. Cast off, Paddington. Hold on everyone! "

" Do what, Mr. Brown? " cried Paddington, above the splashing of the water. Having a picnic on the river was much more complicated than he had expected. There were so many ropes to pull he was getting a bit confused. First of all Mr. Brown had told him to untie the rope. Now he had shouted to everyone to hold on.

Paddington closed his eyes and held on to the rope with both paws as tightly as he could.

He wasn't quite sure what happened next. One moment he was standing on the boat—the next moment it wasn't there any more.

" Henry! " shouted Mrs. Brown, as there was a loud splash. " For goodness' sake! Paddington's fallen in the water! "

"Bear overboard!" cried Jonathan, as the boat shot away from the bank.

"Hold on, Paddington!" called Judy. "We're coming."

"But I *did* hold on," cried Paddington, as he came up spluttering for air. "That's how I fell in."

Mrs. Brown lunged into the water with her sunshade. "Do hurry, Henry," she cried.

"I'm sure Paddington can't swim," said Judy.

"What did you say?" called Paddington.

"She said 'you can't swim,'" yelled Mr. Brown.

When he heard what Mr. Brown said Paddington began waving his paws wildly in the air and there was a gurgle as he promptly sank.

"There now, Henry," exclaimed Mrs. Brown.

"Now look what you've done. He was all right until you spoke."

"I like that!" said Mr. Brown, giving his wife an expressive look.

"It's all right," shouted Jonathan. "Someone's thrown him a lifebelt!"

By the time the Browns reached the landing stage Paddington had already been rescued and he was lying on his back surrounded by a large crowd. Everyone was staring down at him making suggestions while the man in charge of the boats pulled his paws back and forth, giving him artificial respiration.

"Thank goodness he's safe," exclaimed Mrs. Brown thankfully.

"Don't see why 'e shouldn't be," said the man. "If 'e'd layed 'isself down it'd only 'ave come up to 'is whiskers. The water's only about nine inches deep just 'ere. Probably a lot less now—judging by the amount 'e's swallowed. Kept 'is mouth open when 'e went under I dare say."

Judy bent down and looked at Paddington. " I think he's trying to say something," she said.

" Grrrr," said Paddington as he sat up.

" Now just you lay still for a moment, young feller-me-bear," said the boatman, pushing Paddington back down again.

" Grrr," said Paddington. " ITHINKI'VELOST-MYHAT."

" ITHINKI'VELOSTMYHAT," repeated the man, looking at Paddington with renewed interest. " Are you one of they foreign bears? We get a rare lot of overseas visitors at this time of year," he said, turning to the Browns.

" I *come* from Peru," spluttered Paddington, as he got his breath back. " But I *live* at number thirty-two Windsor Gardens in London, and I think I've lost my hat."

" Oh, dear," said Mrs. Brown, clutching her husband's arm. " Did you hear that, Henry? Paddington's lost his hat! "

The Brown family stared at each other in dismay. They often grumbled about Paddington's hat— usually when he wasn't listening—because it was so old. People had a habit of pointing at it when they were out and it made them feel embarrassed. But all the same, they couldn't even begin to picture Paddington without it.

"I had it on when I fell in the water," cried Paddington, feeling on top of his head. "And now it isn't there any more."

"Gosh," said Jonathan. "It had so many holes in it too! Perhaps it's sunk."

"Sunk!" cried Paddington in dismay. He ran to the edge of the landing stage and peered at the muddy water. "But it can't have *sunk*!"

"He's always worn it," explained Mrs. Brown to the boatman. "Ever since we've known him. It was given to him by his uncle in Peru."

"*Darkest* Peru," said Paddington.

"Darkest Peru," repeated the boatman, looking most impressed. He turned to Paddington and touched his forelock. "You'll be wanting the Thames Conservancy, sir."

"No, I don't," said Paddington firmly. "I want my hat."

"He means they look after the river, dear," explained Mrs. Brown. "They may have found it for you."

"It's the current, sir," explained the boatman. "Once you get away from the bank it's very strong and it may have got swep' over the weir." He pointed along the river towards a row of buildings in the distance.

" Got swep' over the weir? " repeated Paddington slowly.

The boatman nodded. " If it ain't already been sucked into a whirlpool."

Paddington gave the man a hard stare. " My hat! " he exclaimed, hardly able to believe his ears. " Got sucked into a whirlpool? "

" Come along," said Mr. Brown hastily. " If we hurry we may be just in time to see it go over."

Closely followed by Mr. and Mrs. Brown, Mrs. Bird, Jonathan and Judy, the boatman and a crowd of interested sightseers, Paddington hurried along the towpath with a grim expression on his face, leaving a trail of water behind him.

By the time they reached the weir the news had already spread and several men in peaked caps were peering anxiously into the water.

" I hear you've lost a very valuable Persian cat," said the lock-keeper to Mr. Brown.

" Not a *cat*," said Mr. Brown. " A *hat*. And it's from Peru."

" It belongs to this young bear gentleman, Fred,"

explained the boatman as he joined
them. "It's a family heirloom."

"A family heirloom?" repeated
the lock-keeper, scratching his
head as he looked at Paddington. "I've never heard
of a hat being a family heirloom before. Especially
a bear's heirloom."

"Mine is," said Paddington firmly. "It's a very
rare sort of hat and it's got a marmalade sandwich

inside. I put it in there in case of an emergency."

"A marmalade sandwich?" said the lock-keeper, looking more and more surprised. "Wait a minute— it wouldn't be that thing we fished out just now would it? All sort of shapeless . . . like a . . . like a . . ." He tried hard to think of words to describe it.

"That *sounds* like it," said Mrs. Bird.

"Herbert!" called the man to a boy who was standing nearby watching the proceedings with an open mouth. "See if we've still got that wassname in the shed."

"It might well be an heirloom," he continued, turning to the Browns. "It looks as if it's been handed down a lot."

Everyone waited anxiously while Herbert disappeared into a small hut by the side of the lock. He returned after a few moments carrying a bucket.

"We put it in here," said the lock-keeper apologetically, "because we'd never seen anything like it before. We were going to send it to the museum."

Paddington peered into the bucket. "That's not a wassname," he exclaimed thankfully. "That's my hat."

Everyone breathed a sigh of relief. "Thank goodness," said Mrs. Bird, echoing all their thoughts.

"There's a fish inside it as well," said the lock-keeper.

"What!" exclaimed Paddington. "A fish? Inside my hat?"

"That's right," said the man. "It must have been after your marmalade sandwich. Probably got in through one of the holes."

"Crikey," exclaimed Jonathan admiringly, as the Browns gathered round the bucket. "So there is!"

"That means Paddington's won the prize for catching the first fish," said Judy. "Congratulations!"

"Well, if it's some kind of competition," said the lock-keeper, "I'd better get you a jam-jar to put it in, sir."

"I suppose," he said, looking rather doubtfully at the hat, "you'll be wanting to wear it again?"

As Paddington gave him a hard stare he backed away and hurried off in search of a jam-jar. "There you are," he said when he returned. "With the compliments of the Thames Conservancy."

"Thank you very much," said Paddington gratefully, offering the man his paw.

"Not at all," said the

man, as he stood on the side of the lock to wave them good-bye. "It's a pleasure. After all, it's not every day we have the opportunity of saving a bear's heir-loom from going over the weir. I shall remember to-day for a long time to come."

"And so shall I remember it," said Mr. Brown as he stopped rowing some while later and let the boat drift lazily downstream in the current. "It may not have been the quietest day we've ever spent on the river, but it's certainly the nicest."

And the Brown family, as they lay back in the boat watching the shimmering water and listening to the music from the gramophone, had to agree.

Paddington, as he held on tightly to his hat with one paw while he dipped the other into a jar of his favourite marmalade, agreed most of all. Now that he had got his hat back and everything had been restored to normal he felt it was quite the nicest day he'd had for a long time.

CHAPTER TWO

Paddington Makes a Bid

PADDINGTON'S FRIEND, Mr. Gruber, laughed no end
when he heard all about the trip on the river.

" Oh, dear, Mr. Brown," he said, wiping the tears
from his eyes, "things do happen to you. I wish I
could have been there to see it all."

It was the morning after the picnic and Paddington
had hurried round as soon as possible to tell Mr.
Gruber all about it.

Mr. Gruber kept an antique shop in the Portobello
Road. It was near the Browns' house and Paddington
usually called in when he was doing the morning
shopping so that they could share a bun and a cup of
cocoa for their " elevenses." In his younger days

25

Mr. Gruber had been to South America and so they were able to have long chats together about Darkest Peru while sitting in their deck-chairs on the pavement. Paddington always looked forward to seeing Mr. Gruber and he often lent a paw around the shop.

Most of the shops in the Portobello Road were interesting, but Mr. Gruber's was the best of all. It was like going into Aladdin's cave. There were swords and old suits of armour hanging on the walls, gleaming copper and brass pots and pans stacked on the floor, pictures, china ornaments, pieces of furniture and pottery piled up to the ceiling; in fact, there was very little one way and another that Mr. Gruber didn't sell, and people came from far and wide to seek his advice.

Mr. Gruber also kept a huge library of second-hand books in the back of his shop which he let Paddington consult whenever any problems cropped up. Paddington found this most useful as the Public Library didn't have a bear's department and the assistants usually looked at him suspiciously when he peered through the window at them.

After Paddington had explained to Mr. Gruber all about his trip on the river they fell silent for a moment while they ate their buns and drank their cocoa.

It was while he was sitting back in his deck-chair admiring the view and watching the passers-by that

Paddington noticed Mr. Gruber's shop window for the first time that morning. To his surprise it looked unusually empty.

"Ah," said Mr. Gruber, following his glance. "I had a very busy day yesterday, Mr. Brown. While you were having high jinks on the river a big party of American visitors came round and they bought all kinds of things.

"As a matter of fact," he continued, "I did so well I have to go to an auction sale this afternoon to pick up some more antiques."

"An auction sale?" said Paddington, looking most interested. "What does it look like, Mr. Gruber?"

Mr. Gruber thought for a moment. "Well," he began, "it's a place where they sell things to the highest bidder, Mr. Brown. All kinds of things. But it's very difficult to explain without actually showing you."

Mr. Gruber rubbed his glasses and coughed. "Er . . . I suppose, Mr. Brown, it wouldn't be possible for you to come along with me this afternoon, would it? Then you could see for yourself."

"Oooh, yes, please, Mr. Gruber," exclaimed Paddington, his eyes gleaming with excitement at the thought. "I should like that very much indeed."

Although they met most days, Mr. Gruber was usually busy in his shop and they seldom had the opportunity of actually going out together.

At that moment a customer entered the shop and so, having arranged to meet Mr. Gruber after lunch, Paddington raised his hat and hurried back home to tell the others.

"Hmm," said Mrs. Bird, when she heard all about it over lunch. "I pity the poor auctioneer who tries to sell anything when Paddington's there. That bear'll knock anyone down to half-price."

"Oh, I'm not *buying* anything, Mrs. Bird," said Paddington, as he reached out a paw for a second helping of treacle tart. "I'm only going to watch."

All the same, when he left the house after lunch, Mrs. Bird noticed he was carrying his old leather suitcase in which he kept all his money.

"It's all right, Mrs. Bird," said Paddington, as he waved good-bye with his paw. "It's only in case of an emergency."

"Just so long as he doesn't come home with a suite of furniture," said Mrs. Bird as she closed the door. "If he does it'll have to go in the garden."

Paddington felt very excited as he entered the auction rooms. Mr. Gruber had put on his best suit for the occasion and a number of people turned to stare at them as they came through the door.

Having bought two catalogues, Mr. Gruber pushed his way to the front so that Paddington would have a good view. On the way he introduced him to several of the other dealers as "Mr. Brown—a young bear friend of mine from Darkest Peru who's interested in antiques."

They all shook Paddington's paw and whispered that they were very pleased to meet him.

It was all much different to what Paddington had expected. It was really like a very big antique shop, with boxes and tables loaded with china and silver round the walls. There was a large crowd of people standing in the middle of the room facing a man on a platform who appeared to be waving a hammer in the air.

" That's the auctioneer," whispered Mr. Gruber. "He's the man you want to watch. He's most important."

Paddington raised his hat politely to the auctioneer and then settled down on his suitcase and carefully looked around.

After a moment he decided he liked auction sales. Everyone seemed so friendly. In fact, he had hardly made himself comfortable before a man on the other side of the room waved his hand in their direction. Paddington stood up, raised his hat and waved a friendly paw back.

No sooner had he sat down than the man waved again. Being a polite bear, Paddington stood up and once more waved his paw.

To his surprise the man stopped waving almost immediately and glared at him instead. Paddington gave him a hard stare and then settled down to watch the man on the platform who appeared to be doing something with his hammer again.

" Going . . ." the man shouted, hitting his table. " Going . . . gone! Sold to the young bear gentleman in the hat for two pounds ten! "

" Oh, dear," said Mr. Gruber, looking most upset. " I'm afraid you've just bought a set of carpentry tools, Mr. Brown."

" *What!* " repeated Paddington, nearly falling off his suitcase with surprise. " *I've bought a set of carpentry tools?* "

" Come along," said the auctioneer sternly. " You're holding up the proceedings. Pay at the desk, please."

"A set of carpentry tools," exclaimed Paddington, jumping up and waving his paws in the air. "But I didn't even say anything!"

Mr. Gruber looked most embarrassed. "I'm afraid it's all my fault, Mr. Brown," he said. "I should have explained auction sales to you before we came in. I think perhaps *I'd* better pay for them as it wasn't really your fault."

"You see," he continued, when he returned from the desk, "you have to be very careful at a sale, Mr. Brown."

Mr. Gruber went on to explain how the auctioneer offered each item for sale, and how, after one person had made a bid for something, it was up to anyone else who wanted it to make a better offer.

"If you nod your head, Mr. Brown," he said, "or even scratch your nose, they think it's a sign you want to buy something. I expect the auctioneer saw you raise your hat just now and thought you were bidding."

Paddington wasn't at all sure what Mr. Gruber meant, but having carefully made sure the auctioneer wasn't looking, he quickly nodded and then sat very still while he watched the proceedings.

Although he didn't say anything to Mr. Gruber, he was beginning to wish he hadn't come to the auction. The room was hot and crowded and he wanted to take his hat off. Apart from that he was sitting on the handle of his suitcase, which was most uncomfortable.

He closed his eyes and was just about to try and go to sleep when Mr. Gruber nudged his paw and pointed to the catalogue.

" I say, Mr. Brown," he said. " The next item is very interesting. It's an old pistol—the sort highwaymen used. They're quite popular just now. I think I shall try bidding for it."

Paddington sat up and watched excitedly as the auctioneer held the pistol in the air for everyone to see. " Lot thirty-four," he shouted. " What am I bid for this genuine antique pistol ? "

" Four pounds," came a voice from the back of the room.

" Four pounds ten," called Mr. Gruber, waving his catalogue.

" Five pounds," came another voice.

" Oh, dear," said Mr. Gruber, making some calculations on the side of his catalogue. " Five pounds ten shillings."

" Six pounds," came the same voice again.

Paddington stood on his case and stared across the room. " That's the man who made me buy the carpentry tools by mistake," he whispered, tapping Mr. Gruber excitedly.

" Well, we mustn't let *him* have it whatever we do," exclaimed Mr. Gruber. " Six pounds ten ! "

" Seven pounds," cried Paddington wildly.

" Ahem," said Mr. Gruber tactfully, not wishing to offend Paddington. " I think we're bidding against each other, Mr. Brown."

" Any advance on seven pounds? " shouted the auctioneer, looking most pleased.

As there was no reply he raised his hammer. " Going . . . going . . ." he called. " Gone! " He brought the hammer down with a loud crash. " Sold to the young bear gentleman in the front row for seven pounds."

Mr. Gruber felt in his wallet for the money. Taking Paddington to an auction sale was becoming rather expensive.

" I'm sorry about that, Mr. Gruber," said Paddington guiltily, when he returned. " I'm afraid I got rather excited."

" That's all right," said Mr. Gruber. " It was still a very good bargain, Mr. Brown—and I did want it. I shall put it in my window to-morrow."

" I think perhaps I'd better not do any more bidding," said Paddington, looking very crestfallen. " I don't think bears are very good at it."

" Nonsense," said Mr. Gruber. " You've been doing very well for a first time."

All the same, Paddington decided to keep quiet for a while and watch Mr. Gruber. It was all very complicated and not a bit like shopping in the market,

where he was allowed to test everything with his
paws first before arguing over the price.

Mr. Gruber pointed out several items in the
catalogue to Paddington and gave him a pencil so
that he could mark off the ones he had bought and
how much had been paid for them.

The list of items Mr. Gruber bought grew and
grew until Paddington felt quite dizzy with writing
down all the figures and he was pleased when at last
he announced that he had finished buying for the day.

"A very good day's work indeed, Mr. Brown," he
said, as he checked Paddington's figures. "And
thank you very much for all your help. I don't know
what I would have done without you."

Paddington looked up from his own catalogue which he had been studying earnestly. " That's all right, Mr. Gruber," he said vaguely. " Excuse me, but what is a preserves stand ? "

" A preserves stand ? " said Mr. Gruber. " Well, it's a thing for holding jam or marmalade."

Paddington's eyes gleamed as he started to unlock his suitcase. " I think I shall bid for that, Mr. Gruber," he said excitedly, as he peered inside the secret compartment to see how much money he had. " It's the next item in the catalogue. I think I should like a preserves stand for my marmalade."

Mr. Gruber looked at him rather nervously. " I should be careful if I were you, Mr. Brown," he said. " It may be an antique one. If it is it's probably worth a lot of money."

But before he had time to explain to Paddington just how much it might cost him the auctioneer rapped on his table for silence.

" Lot 99," he shouted, as he held up a piece of shining silver to the light. " A very unusual kind of preserves stand. What am I bid for this valuable piece of antique silver ? "

" Sixpence! " cried Paddington.

A hush fell over the room. " Sixpence ? " echoed the auctioneer, hardly able to believe his ears. " Did I hear someone say *sixpence* ? "

" I did," called Paddington, waving his catalogue

35

in the air. " I want it to keep my marmalade in. Mrs.
Bird's always grumbling because my jars get sticky."

"Your *jars* get sticky?" repeated the auctioneer,
passing a hand over his forehead. It really was a most
unusual day. Things hadn't gone at all according to
plan. Some items had been sold for far more than he
had ever expected. Others—like this preserves stand
—were fetching nothing at all. He had a nasty feeling
it had something to do with the young bear in the
front row. He seemed to have a very powerful stare
and he'd done his best up to now to avoid catching
Paddington's eye.

" Come, come," he said, giving a high-pitched

laugh. " I'm sure we all enjoy a little joke. Let's start again. Now—what am I bid for this valuable item? "

" Ninepence," said a voice at the back of the hall amid laughter.

" Tenpence," said Paddington firmly.

The laughter died down and there was silence. " If you ask me," whispered a voice behind Paddington, " that young bear knows something."

" It's probably a fake," whispered another voice. " After all—it's not the first thing he's bought this afternoon."

"He's with old Mr. Gruber, too," whispered the first voice. " And he said he was interested in antiques when he came in. I wouldn't touch it if I were you."

The auctioneer shuddered as he gazed at the preserves stand in his hand. "Any advance on tenpence? " he cried.

There was another long silence. " Going . . ." he shouted, raising his hammer and looking around hopefully. " Going . . ." Still no one spoke. " Gone! "

He brought his hammer down on the desk with a crash. " Sold to the young bear gentleman in the front row for tenpence."

" Thank you very much," said Paddington, as he hurried up to the table. " I hope you don't mind if I pay you in ha'pennies but I've been saving up in case of an emergency."

"Ha'pennies?" said the man. He mopped his brow with a spotted handkerchief. "I don't know," he said, turning to his assistant. "I must be getting old. Letting young bears get the better of me at my time of life."

"A very good bargain indeed," said Mr. Gruber admiringly, when they were outside the saleroom. He turned Paddington's preserves stand over in his hands. "I should say it's worth every penny of five pounds."

"Five pounds?" exclaimed Paddington, staring at Mr. Gruber. "Five pounds for a marmalade stand?"

"At least that," said Mr. Gruber. "I'll put it in my window for you if you like, Mr. Brown."

Paddington thought hard for a moment. "I think I would like you to have it as a present, Mr. Gruber," he said at last. "I don't expect you'd have bought the carpentry tools if I hadn't been at the auction sale."

Mr. Gruber looked most affected by Paddington's offer. "That's very kind of you, Mr. Brown," he said. "Very kind of you indeed. But I know how fond you are of marmalade and I'd much rather you had it. Besides," he added, "I've had a very good day and I think it was worth the price of the carpentry tools just to see the expression on the auctioneer's face when you offered him sixpence for the preserves stand."

Mr. Gruber chuckled at the thought. "I don't

think he's had many dealings with young bears before," he said.

"I've said it before," remarked Mrs. Bird, later that evening, "and I'll say it again. That bear's got an eye for a bargain."

The Browns were having a late supper before going to bed. Paddington's "antique" stood in the centre of the table in a place of honour. He had spent most of the evening polishing it until he could see his whiskers in the side and Mrs. Bird had opened a new jar of his favourite marmalade especially for the occasion.

There was a blissful expression on Paddington's face—that part of it which could be seen behind bread and butter crumbs and smears of marmalade.

"I think," he announced, amid general agreement, "preserves taste even nicer when they come out of an antique."

"Especially," he added, as he dipped his paw into the marmalade, "a tenpenny one!"

CHAPTER THREE

Paddington and "Do it Yourself"

PADDINGTON sat up in bed late that night writing his memories. He had a large leather-bound scrap-book given to him by Mr. Gruber in which he kept a record of all his adventures, together with any interesting pictures, and he carefully pasted in the receipt for his tenpence which the auctioneer had given him.

When he did eventually fall asleep it was only to dream he was at the auction sale again. He was standing in the middle of the auction rooms waving his paws and bidding for everything that was offered for sale. The pile of things he'd bought got bigger and bigger as they were placed around him until he could hardly see out. Several of the larger items were sticking in his side.

When he woke he was very relieved to find he was still in his own room and that the banging of the auctioneer's hammer was really only someone knocking at his door.

As he sat up in bed rubbing his eyes Paddington also found to his surprise that the marmalade dish was in bed with him and he had, in fact, been lying on it.

" Paddington! " exclaimed Mrs. Brown, as she entered carrying the breakfast things. " What on earth's the matter? I kept hearing a lot of banging and shouting coming from your room in the night."

" I expect it was the noise of the furniture, Mrs. Brown," explained Paddington, hastily drawing the sheets up round his ears so that she wouldn't see the marmalade stains.

" The furniture? " exclaimed Mrs. Brown, as she put the tray down on the bed. " What furniture? "

" The furniture I bought in my dream," said Paddington patiently.

Mrs. Brown sighed. Sometimes she couldn't make head or tail of what Paddington was talking about. " I've brought you your breakfast in bed," she said, " because Mrs. Bird and I have to go out this morning. We're taking Jonathan and Judy to the dentist and we thought perhaps you wouldn't mind being left on your own. Unless," she added, "you'd like to come too?"

"Oh, no," said Paddington hastily. "I don't think I should like to go to the dentist, thank you very much. I'd much rather stay at home."

"There's a big box arrived from Mr. Gruber," continued Mrs. Brown. "I think it's the carpentry tools you bought in the sale yesterday. I've had them put in the shed."

"Thank you, Mrs. Brown," said Paddington, hoping she would soon go as it was getting very hot under the blankets and the marmalade dish was sticking in his side again.

Mrs. Brown paused in the doorway. "We shan't be any longer than we can help. You're sure you'll be all right?"

"I expect I shall find *something* to do," said Paddington vaguely.

Mrs. Brown hesitated before shutting the door. She would have liked to ask Paddington a few more questions. He had a far-away look in his eyes which she didn't like the look of at all. But she was already late for the appointment, and conversation with Paddington, particularly in the early morning, was liable to become complicated.

When Mrs. Bird heard all about Paddington's strange behaviour she hurried upstairs to see what was going on, but she arrived back a few moments later with the news that he was sitting up in bed eating his breakfast and reading a catalogue.

" Oh, well," said Mrs. Brown, looking most relieved. " He can't come to much harm doing that."

In recent weeks Paddington had begun to collect catalogues and whenever he saw an interesting one advertised in the newspapers he usually sent away for it. In fact, hardly a day went by without the postman calling at least once with a letter addressed to " P. Brown, Esq. "

Some of the catalogues were very good value indeed, full of pictures and drawings, and with quite a lot to read considering they were free and that Mrs. Bird usually paid for the stamp.

Paddington kept them all in a cupboard beside his

bed. There were a number on foreign travel—with pictures of far-away places in several colours; two or three on food; and one or two from some big London stores.

But the one which interested Paddington at the moment, and which was his favourite, showed a work-bench on the front cover and was headed DO IT YOURSELF. He became so absorbed in the booklet, which was a thick one full of diagrams, that he suddenly found to his surprise that he had put the pepper and salt into his cup of tea and the sugar into his boiled egg. But it made quite an interesting taste so he didn't really mind and he concentrated on reading the catalogue over his toast and marmalade.

There was a particularly interesting section which caught his eye. It was headed DELIGHT YOUR FAMILY AND SURPRISE YOUR FRIENDS, and it was all about making a newspaper and magazine rack.

"All you need," it said, " is a sheet of plywood, some nails, and a kitchen table."

Paddington wasn't at all sure about using Mrs. Bird's kitchen table, but the night before Mr. Brown had rashly promised him a sheet of plywood that was standing in the shed, as well as some old nails in a jam-jar. And Mr. Brown was always grumbling about not being able to find his newspapers; Paddington felt sure he would be very pleased if he had a rack for them.

He examined the drawings and pictures carefully and consulted the instructions several times. It didn't say anything about bears in particular doing it themselves, but it did say it was suitable for anyone with a set of carpentry tools.

Paddington came to a decision. He hastily wrapped the remains of his breakfast in a handkerchief in case the sawing made him hungry. Then, having marked the chapter on magazine racks in his catalogue with a piece of marmalade peel, he hurried along to the bathroom for a quick wash.

Paddington wasn't the sort of bear who believed in doing things unnecessarily and it wasn't worth having a proper wash if he was going to get dirty again. After passing the face flannel over his whiskers a couple of times he made his way downstairs and went out into the garden.

The box of carpentry tools was standing in the middle of Mr. Brown's shed and Paddington spent several minutes investigating it. Although all the tools seemed rather large for a bear he soon decided he was very pleased with them. There was a hammer, a plane, three chisels, a large saw and a number of other things which he didn't immediately recognise but which looked very interesting. The box was heavy and it took him some while to drag it outside into the garden. He had even more trouble with Mr. Brown's plywood, for it was a large sheet and there was a wind blowing.

Each time he picked it up a gust of wind caught it and carried him farther and farther down the garden.

It was while he was trying to drag it back up again with the aid of a piece of rope that he heard a familiar voice calling his name. He looked round and saw Mr. Curry, the Browns' next-door neighbour, watching him over the fence. Mr. Curry didn't approve of bears and he usually viewed Paddington's "goings on" with suspicion.

"What are you doing, bear?" he growled.

"Do it yourself, Mr. Curry," said Paddington, peering out from behind the sheet of wood.

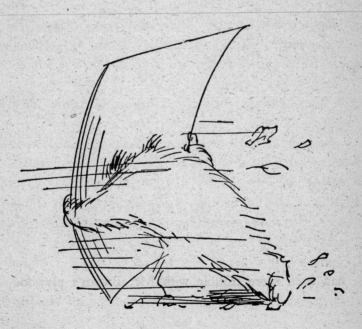

"What?" bellowed Mr. Curry. "Don't be impertinent, bear!"

"Oh, no," said Paddington hastily, nearly dropping the sheet of plywood in his fright at the expression on Mr. Curry's face. "I didn't mean you were to do it *yourself*, Mr. Curry. I meant I'm going to do it *myself*. I'm making a magazine rack for Mr. Brown."

"A magazine rack?" repeated Mr. Curry.

"Yes," said Paddington importantly, and he began explaining to Mr. Curry all about his new carpentry set.

As he listened to Paddington the expression on Mr. Curry's face gradually changed. Mr. Curry had a reputation in the neighbourhood for meanness and he was always on the look-out in the hope of getting something for nothing. He was very keen on doing things himself, too, in order to save money, and he cast several envious glances at Paddington's tool set.

"Hmm," he said, when Paddington had finished. "And where are you going to make this magazine rack, bear? On the lawn?"

"Well," said Paddington doubtfully, "It's a bit difficult. It says in the instructions I'm supposed to have a kitchen table and Mrs. Bird's is full up."

"Hmm," said Mr. Curry once again. "If I let you make me a magazine rack, bear, you can use *my* kitchen table."

"Thank you very much, Mr. Curry," said Paddington. But he wasn't sure whether it was a good idea or not and he looked at Mr. Curry rather doubtfully. "That's most kind of you."

"I have to go out this morning," said Mr. Curry. "So you can have it ready for me when I get back.

"Mind you," he added, as he reached over the fence to give Paddington a hand with the plywood, "I'm not having any sawdust over the kitchen floor. And mind you don't scratch anything."

The more he listened to Mr. Curry talking the longer Paddington's face grew and he was glad when at last he left to do his shopping.

But as Paddington set to work he soon forgot all about Mr. Curry's list of "don'ts," for there were a number of important things to be done. First of all he took a pencil and ruler and carefully marked out the shape of the magazine rack on the sheet of plywood. Then he placed this on top of the kitchen table, ready to be sawn in two.

Paddington had never actually sawn anything be-

49

fore, but he'd often watched Mr. Brown cutting up logs
for the fire. From a safe distance it had always looked
easy—but Paddington soon found it wasn't easy at
all. To start with the plywood was bigger than the
top of Mr. Curry's table. Being small, Paddington
had to climb on top of it and several times it nearly
tipped over when he stood too near the edge. Then
he found that the saw, although it was nice and sharp,
was so large he had to use both paws, which made
things even more difficult. For the first few strokes
it went through the wood like a knife through butter,
but for some reason or other it gradually became harder
and harder to use.

After sitting down for a short rest Paddington
decided to try starting from the other end. But once
again, for some strange reason, he found it much
easier at the beginning. However, as he gave the
last saw cut and scrambled clear he was pleased to
see the two saw cuts met in the middle, dividing the
sheet of plywood neatly in half.

It was then, as he reached up to take the newly sawn
pieces of plywood down, that Paddington had his
first shock of the morning.

There was a loud splintering noise and he dodged
back just in time to avoid being hit by Mr. Curry's
table as it suddenly parted in the middle and fell with
a crash to the floor.

Paddington sat in the middle of the kitchen floor

with a mournful expression on his face for quite some time, surveying the wreckage and trying to think of a good reason why Mr. Curry would like two small tables with only two legs each instead of one big one with four legs.

He consulted the instructions in his catalogue hopefully several times, but there didn't seem to be anything about mending tables which had accidentally been sawn in half. In all the pictures the people seemed to be happy and smiling and their kitchens were as shiny as a new pin. Whereas, looking unhappily around Mr. Curry's kitchen, even Paddington had to admit it was in a bit of a mess.

He tried propping the two pieces of table up on some old cardboard boxes, but there was still a nasty sag in the middle, and even with the curtains drawn and the light out it was obvious something was wrong.

Paddington was a hopeful bear in many ways and he suddenly remembered seeing a large tube of glue in his carpentry set. If he spread some of the glue along the two edges and nailed them together for good measure, perhaps even Mr. Curry might not notice anything was wrong. He worked hard for some minutes and by the time he had finished he felt quite pleased with himself. Admittedly the table had a funny tilt to one side and seemed a trifle wobbly, but it was definitely in one piece again. He spread some flour over the join and then stood back to admire his handiwork.

Having carefully examined it from all angles, he decided he might be able to improve matters still further by sawing a piece off one of the legs. But when he had done that the table seemed to lean the opposite way—which meant he had to saw a piece off one of the other legs as well. Then, when he had done that, he discovered the table was leaning the other way again.

Paddington gave a deep sigh. Carpentry was much more difficult than it looked. He was sure the man in the catalogue didn't have so much trouble.

It was after he had been at work for some time that he stood up and received his second shock of the morning.

When he had first started sawing the legs, Mr. Curry's table had been as tall as he was. Now he found he was looking down at it. In fact, he didn't remember ever having seen such a short table before and his eyes nearly popped out with astonishment.

He sat down on the pile of sawn-off table legs and consulted his catalogue once again.

" Delight your family and surprise your friends! " he said bitterly, to the world in general. He was quite sure Mr. Curry would be surprised when he saw his kitchen table, but as for anyone being delighted

by their magazine racks—he hadn't even started
work on those yet.

Mrs. Brown looked anxiously at the dining-room
clock. " I wonder where on earth Paddington can
have got to," she said. " It's almost lunch time and
it's most unlike him to be late for a meal."

"Perhaps he's doing a job somewhere," said
Jonathan. " I looked in the shed just now and that
new tool box of his has disappeared."

"*And* that sheet of plywood Daddy gave him," said Judy.

"Oh, dear," said Mrs. Brown. "I do hope he hasn't built himself in anywhere and can't get out. You know what he's like."

"I don't know about Paddington building himself in," exclaimed Mrs. Bird, as she entered carrying a trayload of plates. "I think Mr. Curry must be having his house pulled down. I've never heard so much noise. Banging and sawing coming from the kitchen. It's been going on ever since we got back and it's only just this minute stopped."

Jonathan and Judy exchanged glances. Now that Mrs. Bird mentioned it, there had been a lot of noise coming from Mr. Curry's house.

"I wonder . . ." said Judy.

Jonathan opened his mouth, but before he had time to say anything the door burst open and Paddington entered dragging something large and heavy behind him.

"Well," said Mrs. Bird, voicing all their thoughts. "And what have you been up to now?"

"What have I been *up* to, Mrs. Bird?" exclaimed Paddington, looking most offended. "I've been making Mr. Brown a magazine rack."

"A magazine rack?" said Mrs. Brown, as Paddington stepped to one side. "What a lovely idea."

" It was meant to be a surprise," said Paddington modestly. " I made it all with my own paws."

" Gosh! It's super," said Jonathan, as the Browns all crowded round to admire Paddington's handiwork. " Fancy you doing it all by yourself."

" I should be careful," warned Paddington. " I've only just varnished it and it's still a bit sticky. I think some of it has come off on my paws already."

" Most sensible," said Mrs. Bird approvingly. "Mentioning no names—it's about time some people in this house had a place for their newspapers. Now perhaps they won't keep losing them."

" But you've made two," said Judy. " Whose is the other one?"

A guilty expression came over Paddington's face. " It's really for Mr. Curry," he said. " But I thought perhaps I'd better leave it on his doorstep after dark —just in case."

Mrs. Bird looked at Paddington suspiciously. Her ears had caught the sound of violent banging coming from the house next door and she had a nasty feeling in the back of her mind that it had something to do with Paddington.

" Just in case?" she repeated. " What do you mean?"

But before Paddington had time to explain exactly what he did mean, Mrs. Brown pointed to the window in astonishment.

"Good gracious," she cried. "There *is* Mr. Curry. Whatever's the matter with him? He's running around the garden waving a kitchen table in the air." She peered through the glass. "And it doesn't seem to have any legs, either. How very odd!"

"Gosh!" cried Jonathan excitedly. "Now it's broken in two!"

The Browns stared through the window at the strange sight of Mr. Curry dancing round his pond waving the two halves of a table. "Bear!" he shouted. "Where are you, bear?"

"Oh, dear," said Paddington, as everyone turned away from the window and looked at him accusingly. "I'm in trouble again."

"Well, if you ask me," said Mrs. Bird, after he had explained everything to them, "the best thing you can do is offer Mr. Curry your carpentry set as a present. Then, perhaps, he'll forget all about his kitchen table. And if he doesn't, just you tell him to come and see me."

Mrs. Bird held very strong views about people who tried to take advantage of others and she usually took Paddington's side in anything to do with Mr. Curry.

"Anyway," she concluded, in a voice which left no room for argument. "I'm certainly not having the lunch spoiled by Mr. Curry or anyone else, so just you all sit down while I fetch it."

With that argument the Browns had to agree and they meekly arranged themselves round the table.

Paddington in particular thought it was a very good idea. He was a bit fed up with carpentry. Sawing was hard work—especially for a small bear—and even more so when it was sawing through a kitchen table. Besides, he was hungry after his morning's work and he didn't want to offend Mrs. Bird by not eating her lunch down to the very last mouthful.

CHAPTER FOUR

A Visit to the Cinema

" I'M AFRAID," said the lady in the cash desk at the
Podium Super Cinema, "you can't come in. It's an
' A ' film."

" I beg your pardon? " said Paddington, looking
puzzled.

" ' A '," said the lady.

" Eh? " repeated Paddington, looking even more
puzzled. " But that's what I said."

" Not ' eh '," said the lady impatiently. " ' A.'
That means bears under sixteen aren't allowed in
unaccompanied."

58

"Sixteen!" exclaimed Paddington, hardly able to believe his ears. "*Sixteen!* But I'm only two. That's another fourteen years. I might not even want to come then."

"Well, that's the law," said the lady sternly. She looked down with some distaste at the top of Paddington's hat. It still had one or two pieces of river weed sticking to it and the warmth of the cinema was bringing out the smell. "Now, come along, please," she said hastily. "You're holding up the queue."

"And no coming back later on wearing long trousers," she called as Paddington turned to go. "I know all the tricks."

Paddington felt most disappointed as he made his way slowly across the foyer. There was a nice warm feeling about the cinema and he particularly liked the way his feet sank into the thick pile of the carpet. After staring hungrily at the sweet counter for a few moments he made his way towards the entrance, giving the attendant a hard stare as the man held the door open for him.

Paddington had never been to the pictures before. In fact he wasn't at all sure what they were. But he enjoyed anything new and for some weeks he had been saving hard out of the one and sixpence a week bun money Mr. Brown gave him, in case an interesting programme came along.

Paddington was a bear who liked getting his

59

money's worth and he'd carefully studied the advertisements outside the Podium until this week, when there was a "Super Double Feature" programme showing —with two long films, a cartoon and a newsreel. Not only that, but a notice outside said there was a special added attraction that evening when Reginald Clove would be playing the theatre organ during the intervals.

Paddington hung about outside the cinema for

several minutes breathing heavily on the glass until he caught sight of a policeman watching him suspiciously and then he hurried home. It was all most disappointing and his carefully saved one and nine-pence was burning a hole in his duffle coat pocket.

"Do you mean to say you've never been to the pictures, Paddington?" said Mr. Brown over tea that afternoon.

"*Never*," said Paddington firmly, as he helped himself to a crumpet. "And now I can't go for another fourteen years unless I'm accompanied."

Mr. Brown looked at his wife. "It's a long time since we all went to the pictures, Mary," he said. "And it's still quite early. Shall we go?"

"Gosh, Dad—let's!" exclaimed Jonathan and Judy together.

"Do you think it's a good programme, Paddington?" asked Mrs. Brown.

"Very good, Mrs. Brown," said Paddington knowledgeably. "There's a cowboy film and a cartoon and an 'I beg your pardon film' as well."

"A *what* film?" exclaimed Mr. Brown.

"An 'I beg your pardon film'," repeated Paddington. "That means bears under sixteen aren't allowed in by themselves."

"Oh, you mean an 'A' film," said Jonathan.

"That's right," agreed Paddington. "That's what I said."

The Browns looked at one another. Sometimes it was a bit difficult explaining things to Paddington.

"*And* there's a man playing the organ," continued Paddington. "It's a special attraction—so I think it's a very good bargain, Mr. Brown."

"That settles it," said Mr. Brown, looking at his watch. "It all sounds much too good to miss."

Immediately the whole house was in an uproar.

Paddington was sent upstairs by Mrs. Bird to wash the crumpet stains off his whiskers while the rest of the family hurried off to their respective rooms to change.

Paddington felt very superior some half an hour later when they all trooped into the Podium Cinema. He raised his hat to the doorkeeper and then led Mr. Brown in the direction of the cash desk.

" I'm accompanied now," he called out to the lady in charge.

The lady stared at Mr. Brown. " I beg your pardon? " she exclaimed. She sniffed and gave him a very strange look. It was most odd but she could distinctly smell fish again.

" What did you say? " she repeated.

" Nothing," said Mr. Brown hastily. " Er . . . I'd like three and three halves for the front row of the circle, please."

" Hurry up, Dad," called Jonathan. " I think the other programme's nearly finished."

Leaving the lady in the cash desk looking most upset, Mr. Brown gathered up a long string of tickets and joined the rest of the family as they hurried up the stairs leading to the circle.

They went up and up and Paddington soon lost count of the number of steps. In fact there were so many he almost wished they had gone downstairs instead. Not only that, but as he followed the Browns through the entrance to the circle he discovered it was all dark inside.

"This way, please," said the usherette, as she led the way down some stairs and shone her torch along a row of seats in the front row. "You're lucky. There are just six left together."

"Thank you very much," said Mrs. Brown, as she made her way along the row. "Excuse me, please. Excuse me. Thank you very much."

She sat down and arranged herself comfortably as the others joined her.

"That's a bit of luck," whispered Mr. Brown. "Finding six together."

"Seven," said Mrs. Brown. "There's still another one between us."

"So there is!" whispered Mr. Brown, groping in the dark. "That's odd. The girl said there were only six." He looked along the row. "Where's Paddington?"

"Paddington?" exclaimed Mrs. Brown. "Isn't he with you, Henry?"

"No," replied Mr. Brown. "I thought *you* had him."

"Oh, crumbs," groaned Judy. "Trust Paddington to get lost."

"Where on earth can he have got to?" grumbled Mr. Brown as he struck a match and began looking under the seats.

" Here I am, Mr. Brown," called Paddington from the end of the row. " I went all the way along by mistake."

" Sssh! " said a nasty sounding voice from the row behind.

" It's all dark and I can't see," exclaimed Paddington as he was passed back along the row.

" Are you all right now, dear? " whispered Mrs. Brown, as Paddington sat down beside her.

" I think so," said Paddington, peering at the screen.

" Oi! " said the nasty voice from behind again. " 'Ow about taking yer titfer off? "

Paddington turned and stared in the direction of the speaker. " My titfer? " he exclaimed. " Take my *titfer* off? "

" That's right," said the voice. " Your tit for tat."

" I think he means your hat, dear," explained Mrs. Brown. " It's probably getting in the way of the screen."

Paddington thought for a moment. He wasn't at all keen on taking his hat off in case it got lost in the dark. " I'll turn it round if you like," he said generously. " Then you can look through one of the holes."

Having solved the problem of the man behind, Paddington gave his attention to the screen. It was all very interesting, with people dashing about all

64

over the place and with music that got louder and louder, but Paddington found it difficult to understand what it was all about. To his surprise, after only a few minutes the music suddenly ended and all the lights in the cinema came on.

" Well," he exclaimed, looking most disappointed. " I didn't think much of that! "

" It's all right, Paddington," explained Judy. " That's what's showing *next* week. That was only the trailer."

But her words fell on empty ears for Paddington was staring at the screen again and licking his whiskers.

" Oh, dear," groaned Mr. Brown, as he followed Paddington's gaze. " They *would* have to advertise ice-cream. They must have known he was coming." He felt in his pocket. " You'd better get six tubs, and some nougat or something for the big picture, Jonathan."

" I think I'm going to enjoy myself," announced Paddington a few minutes later as Mr. Brown handed him the refreshments.

He dipped his spoon into the ice-cream tub and stared excitedly at the screen as the lights went down again to herald the start of the cowboy film.

Paddington enjoyed the cowboy film much more than the trailer, and he soon became quite lost in the story. He stood up on his seat with his paws on the balcony and his eyes glued to the screen. Every now and then he automatically dipped his spoon into the ice-cream tub and several times a lump fell off the spoon before it had even reached his mouth, which was most unusual.

It was all very complicated at first. Everyone seemed to be shooting at everyone else and Paddington got very worried in case there was no one left and they had to stop the film.

Each time the villain, who wore a black mask and a black hat, came on to the screen he booed, and when the hero appeared, riding a white horse, he cheered and waved his hat in the air until Mrs. Brown became quite embarrassed. She wasn't at all sorry when at long last the hero rode off into the setting sun and the film came to an end.

"Most enjoyable," said Mrs. Bird, rather surprisingly. The Browns had somehow never thought of Mrs. Bird liking cowboy films. "Did you like it, Paddington?"

Paddington nodded his head vigorously. "I enjoyed it very much, thank you, Mrs. Bird," he said. "Except I can't find my nougat anywhere."

"Never mind, Paddington," said Mr. Brown, after they had all searched in vain for it. "I'll buy you some more in a minute. *After* we've heard the organ."

He sat back heavily in his seat and then turned to

66

Paddington. "If you watch," he explained, "you'll see it come up through the floor in a moment."

"Come up through the floor, Mr. Brown?" exclaimed Paddington. "I don't think I've ever seen an organ come up through the floor before."

"Oh, dear," said Mrs. Bird. "And it doesn't look as if you're going to now. Look!"

She pointed to the screen where an announcement had just been flashed on to say that Mr. Reginald Clove was indisposed.

"What!" cried Paddington hotly as the words sank in. "Reginald Clove indisposed!"

"That means he's ill, dear," explained Mrs. Brown. "So he won't be playing after all."

"How very disappointing," said Mr. Brown. "It's a long time since I heard an organ. I was really looking forward to it."

While the rest of the Browns watched the advertisements on the screen Paddington sank back into his seat and listened to Mr. Brown explaining what the organ would have looked like had it come up through the floor. Mr. Brown liked organs and he went on for a long time about it.

"Henry," said Mrs. Brown when he had finished. "Where's Paddington?"

"Paddington?" exclaimed Mr. Brown. "Don't tell me he's disappeared *again*. He was here a moment ago."

67

"I do hope he isn't long wherever he's got to," said Mrs. Brown. "We shall never hear the last of it if he misses the start of the big picture."

But Paddington was already almost out of sight. He was hurrying up the aisle and out through the door marked EXIT. There was a purposeful expression on his face, one which the Browns would have recognised at once had they been able to see him.

Paddington wasn't the only one with a purposeful expression on his face at that moment. As he hurried down the stairs on one side of the cinema the manager of the Podium strode up the stairs leading to the projection box on the other.

There was something unusual going on in his

theatre and he intended finding out what it was. He
prided himself that the Podium was normally a very
well run cinema but on this particular evening things
had gone wrong from the beginning.

First of all the lady in the cash desk—usually a
most reliable person—had complained of a fishy smell
and mysterious voices saying they were accompanied
coming from underneath her counter. Then Reginald
Clove had caught his hand in a swing door and had
announced the fact that he couldn't play the organ.

Something to do with his not being able to work the stops and turn the music with only one hand.

As if that wasn't enough there had come news of " goings on " in the circle. It was most unusual to have " goings on " in the circle. Occasionally he had a spot of bother in the cheaper seats downstairs—but never in the circle.

There had been complaints of bear's boos coming from the front row during the cowboy film, and as he'd passed through the stalls he'd also noticed several people immediately underneath the balcony with ice-cream stains on their hats. It was all very disturbing and he wasn't in the best of moods as he burst into the projection room waving a piece of paper.

" I want this notice flashed on the screen," he said crossly. " At once! "

" Good heavens! " exclaimed Mrs. Brown a few moments later. " What on earth can that mean? "

Mr. Brown adjusted his glasses and stared at the screen. " WILL THE OWNER OF THE YOUNG BEAR IN THE CIRCLE KINDLY REPORT TO THE MANAGER'S OFFICE IMMEDIATELY," he read.

" I don't know, Mary," he said, as he made to get to his feet, " but I'm certainly going to find out."

" Owner indeed! " snorted Mrs. Bird. " As if anyone *owned* Paddington."

" The boot's on the other paw, if you ask me,"

began Mr. Brown. "Paddington owns *us*." As he was speaking a strange expression came over his face.

"Well, Henry," said Mrs. Brown, staring at her husband, "aren't you going to do something about it?"

"I . . . I can't get up," exclaimed Mr. Brown, feeling his seat. "I seem to be stuck to something . . . Nougat!" he said bitterly. "Paddington's nougat! No wonder the manager wants to see me in his office."

Unaware of all the excitement that was going on, Paddington pushed open a door and made his way down the aisle of the stalls until he came across a girl selling ice-cream.

"Excuse me," he said, climbing up on to a seat and tapping her on the shoulder, "can you tell me where the indisposed man is?"

"The *indisposed* man?" repeated the girl.

"That's right," said Paddington patiently. "The one who's supposed to come up through the floor."

"Oh, you mean the organist," said the girl. "Mr. Reginald Clove. He's through that little door there. The one under the stage."

Before she could explain that no one was allowed through it without permission Paddington had disappeared again.

Mr. Reginald Clove looked quite startled when Paddington came through the door. He had been expecting *someone* to come, but he certainly hadn't expected it to be a bear.

" Are you from the first aid? " he asked, looking at Paddington rather doubtfully.

" Oh, no," said Paddington, politely raising his hat. " I'm from number thirty-two Windsor Gardens and I've come about the organ."

Mr. Clove stepped back a pace. " You've come about the organ? " he repeated, trying to humour Paddington.

" Yes," said Paddington. " I wanted to see it come up through the floor."

" Oh! " Mr. Clove's face cleared. " Is that all? "

" All! " exclaimed Paddington hotly. " It's very important. Mr. Brown was looking forward to it."

" Oh, dear," said Mr. Clove, idly sorting through a pile of music with his good hand. " I'm so sorry. I wish I could oblige. But I've hurt my hand, you see, and I've no one to turn the music for me, and . . ." He looked thoughtfully at Paddington. " Do *you* like music, bear? " he asked suddenly.

" Oh, yes," replied Paddington. " But I don't really play anything except the comb and paper and I'm not very good at that because I get my whiskers caught in the comb."

" Do you think you could turn the music for me? " asked Mr. Clove.

" Well," said Paddington doubtfully, " it's a bit

difficult for bears because of their paws, but if you could tell me when to do it I could try."

Mr. Clove came to a decision. " You'll do," he said briskly. " Come with me."

" *Goings on!* " exclaimed Mrs. Bird, waving her handbag at the manager. " They weren't ' goings on.' He was only enjoying himself."

" Bear's boos," said the manager sternly. " In the Podium circle. And nougat on one of my best seats."

" Then you shouldn't sell it," replied Mrs. Bird. " It's asking for trouble."

" Well, where is he now? " demanded the manager. " Tell me that. I want to start the big picture. We're five minutes late already."

The Browns exchanged anxious glances. Knowing Paddington he might be anywhere, but before they had time to reply they were all startled into silence by a loud rumbling from the front of the cinema which grew and grew in volume until the whole place began to shake.

" Good heavens! " exclaimed the manager as a burst of applause swept through the audience. " It's Reginald Clove playing ' Rule Britannia! ' And with one hand, too! "

They all stared over the balcony as the lights dimmed and the organ rose into view bathed in a pink spotlight.

" Mercy me," cried Mrs. Bird, clutching her seat. " And there's that bear—what on earth is he doing now? "

Paddington felt most important as he rode up on the organ and he wished he could turn and wave to the Browns to let them know where he was, but he was much too busy carrying out Mr. Clove's instructions.

Even so, there was one nasty moment when, in his excitement, he turned over two pages of music at once by mistake. Mr. Clove looked most surprised when he suddenly found himself playing a selection from *The Gondoliers* instead of " Rule Britannia," but he quickly recovered and in the general excitement no one seemed to notice.

The audience applauded all the items and Paddington felt quite sorry when Mr. Clove at last pressed a button by his side and the organ began to sink back through the floor. But as it finally disappeared from view and the last notes of the music died away a loud cheer went up from the audience and several voices were heard shouting for more.

Afterwards everyone agreed that good though the big picture was, the organ had been the high spot of the evening. Even the manager of the Podium seemed very pleased and he took the Browns on a tour behind the scenes before they left.

" I don't suppose," said Paddington thoughtfully,

as they made their way home, " there are many bears who've been for a ride on an organ. Especially one that comes up through the floor."

"And I don't suppose," said Mr. Brown, as he turned and looked hard at Paddington, " that there are many people who've been stuck to their seat by a piece of bear's nougat."

But Paddington had his eyes closed. He wasn't exactly asleep, but he had a lot of things to write in his scrap-book that night when he went to bed. He'd enjoyed his visit to the pictures and it needed a lot of careful thought to put it all into words.

CHAPTER FIVE

Something Nasty in the Kitchen

"Two DAYS!" exclaimed Mrs. Brown, staring at Doctor MacAndrew in horror. "Do you mean to say we've to stay in bed for two whole days?"

"Aye," said Doctor MacAndrew, "there's a nasty wee bug going the rounds and if ye don't I'll no' be responsible for the consequences."

"But Mrs. Bird's away until to-morrow," said Mrs. Brown. "And so are Jonathan and Judy . . . and . . . and that only leaves Paddington."

"Two days," repeated Doctor MacAndrew as he snapped his bag shut. "And not a moment less. The house'll no' fall down in that time."

" There's one thing," he added, as he paused at the door and stared at Mr. and Mrs. Brown with a twinkle in his eye. " Whatever else happens you'll no die of starvation. Yon wee bear's verra fond of his inside! "

With that he went downstairs to tell Paddington the news.

" Oh, dear," groaned Mr. Brown, as the door closed behind the doctor. " I think I feel worse already."

Paddington felt most important as he listened to what Doctor MacAndrew had to say and he carefully wrote down all the instructions. After he had shown him to the door and waved good-bye he hurried back into the kitchen to collect his shopping basket on wheels.

Usually with Paddington shopping in the market was a very leisurely affair. He liked to stop and have a chat with the various traders in the Portobello Road, where he was a well-known figure. To have Paddington's custom was considered to be something of an honour as he had a very good eye for a bargain. But on this particular morning he hardly had time even to call in at the bakers for his morning supply of buns.

It was early and Mr. Gruber hadn't yet opened his shutters, so Paddington wrapped one of the hot buns in a piece of paper, wrote a message on the outside saying who it was from and explaining that he wouldn't be along for " elevenses " that morning, and then pushed it through the letter-box.

Having finished the shopping and been to the chemist with Doctor MacAndrew's prescription, Paddington made his way quickly back to number thirty-two Windsor Gardens.

It wasn't often Paddington had a chance to lend a paw around the house, let alone cook the dinner, and he was looking forward to it. In particular, there was a new feather duster of Mrs. Bird's he'd had his eye on for several days and which he was anxious to test.

" I must say Paddington looks very professional in that old apron of Mrs. Bird's," said Mrs. Brown later that morning. She sat up in bed holding a cup and saucer. " And it was kind of him to bring us up a cup of coffee."

" Very kind," agreed Mr. Brown. " But I rather wish he hadn't brought all these sandwiches as well."

" They *are* rather thick," agreed Mrs. Brown, looking at one doubtfully. " He said they were emergency ones. I'm not quite sure what he meant by that. I do hope nothing's wrong."

" I don't like the sound of it," said Mr. Brown. " There've been several nasty silences this morning— as if something were going on." He sniffed. " And there seems to be a strong smell of burnt feathers coming from somewhere."

" Well, you'd better eat them, Henry," warned

Mrs. Brown. "He's used some of his special marmalade from the cut-price grocer and I'm sure they're meant to be a treat. You'll never hear the last of it if you leave any."

"Yes, but *six*!" grumbled Mr. Brown. "I'm not even very keen on marmalade. And at twelve o'clock in the morning! I shan't want any lunch." He looked thoughtfully at the window and then at the plate of sandwiches again.

"No, Henry," said Mrs. Brown, reading his thoughts. "You're not giving any to the birds. I don't suppose they like marmalade."

"Anyway," she added, "Paddington did say something about lunch being late, so you may be glad of them."

She looked wistfully at the door. "All the same, I wish I could see what's going on. It's not knowing that's the worst part. He had flour all over his whiskers when he came up just now."

"If you ask me," said Mr. Brown, "you're probably much better off being in the dark." He took a long drink from his cup and then jumped up in bed, spluttering.

"Henry, dear," exclaimed Mrs. Brown. "*Do* be careful. You'll have coffee all over the sheets."

"Coffee!" yelled Mr. Brown. "Did you say this was coffee?"

"*I* didn't, dear," said Mrs. Brown mildly. "Paddington did." She took a sip from her own cup and then made a wry face. " It *has* got rather an unusual taste."

" Unusual! " exclaimed Mr. Brown. " It tastes like nothing on earth." He glared at his cup and then poked at it gingerly with a spoon. " It's got some funny green things floating in it too! " he exclaimed.

" Have a marmalade sandwich," said Mrs. Brown. " It'll help take the taste away."

Mr. Brown gave his wife an expressive look. " Two days! " he said, sinking back into the bed. " Two whole days! "

Downstairs, Paddington was in a bit of a mess. So, for that matter was the kitchen, the hall, the dining-room and the stairs.

Things hadn't really gone right since he'd lifted up a corner of the dining-room carpet in order to sweep some dust underneath and had discovered a number of very interesting old newspapers. Paddington sighed. Perhaps if he hadn't spent so much time reading the newspapers he might not have hurried quite so much over the rest of the dusting. Then he might have been more careful when he shook Mrs. Bird's feather duster over the boiler.

And if he hadn't set fire to Mrs. Bird's feather duster he might have been able to take more time over the coffee.

Paddington felt very guilty about the coffee and he rather wished he had tested it before taking it upstairs to Mr. and Mrs. Brown. He was very glad he'd decided to make cocoa for himself instead.

Quite early in the morning Paddington had run out of saucepans. It was the first big meal he had ever

cooked and he wanted it to be something special. Having carefully consulted Mrs. Bird's cookery book he'd drawn out a special menu in red ink with a bit of everything on it.

But by the time he had put the stew to boil in one big saucepan, the potatoes in another saucepan, the peas in a third, the brussels sprouts in yet another, and used at least four more for mixing operations, there was really only the electric kettle left in which to put the cabbage. Unfortunately, in his haste to make the

81

coffee, Paddington had completely forgotten to take the cabbage out again.

Now he was having trouble with the dumplings!

Paddington was very keen on stew, especially when it was served with dumplings, but he was beginning to wish he had decided to cook something else for lunch.

Even now he wasn't quite sure what had gone wrong. He'd looked up the chapter on dumplings in Mrs. Bird's cookery book and followed the instructions most carefully; putting two parts of flour to one of suet and then adding milk before stirring the whole lot together. But somehow, instead of the mixture turning into neat balls as it showed in the coloured picture, it had all gone runny. Then, when he'd added more flour and suet, it had gone lumpy instead and stuck to his fur, so that he'd had to add more milk and then more flour and suet, until he had a huge mountain of dumpling mixture in the middle of the kitchen table.

All in all, he decided, it just wasn't his day. He wiped his paws carefully on Mrs. Bird's apron and, after looking around in vain for a large enough bowl, scraped the dumpling mixture into his hat.

It was a lot heavier than he had expected and he had a job lifting it up on to the stove. It was even more difficult putting the mixture into the stew as it kept sticking to his paws and as fast as he got it off one paw

it stuck to the other. In the end he had to sit on the draining board and use the broom handle.

Paddington wasn't very impressed with Mrs. Bird's cookery book. The instructions seemed all wrong. Not only had the dumplings been difficult to make, but the ones they showed in the picture were much too small. They weren't a bit like the ones Mrs. Bird usually served. Even Paddington rarely managed more than two of Mrs. Bird's dumplings.

Having scraped the last of the mixture off his paws Paddington pushed the saucepan lid hard down and scrambled clear. The steam from the saucepan had made his fur go soggy and he sat in the middle of the floor for several minutes getting his breath back and mopping his brow with an old dish-cloth.

It was while he was sitting there, scraping the remains of the dumplings out of his hat and licking the spoon, that he felt something move behind him. Not only that, but out of the corner of his eye he could see a shadow on the floor which definitely hadn't been there a moment before.

Paddington sat very still, holding his breath and listening. It wasn't so much a noise as a feeling, and it seemed to be creeping nearer and nearer, making a soft swishing noise as it came. Paddington felt his fur begin to stand on end as there came the sound of a slow plop . . . plop . . . plop across the kitchen floor. And then, just as he was summoning up enough courage to look over his shoulder, there was a loud crash from the direction of the stove. Without waiting to see what it was Paddington pulled his hat down over his head and ran, slamming the door behind him.

He arrived in the hall just as there was a loud knock on the front door. To his relief he heard a familiar voice call his name through the letter-box.

" I got your message, Mr. Brown—about not being able to come for elevenses this morning," began Mr. Gruber, as Paddington opened the door, " and I just thought I would call round to see if there was anything I could do . . ." His voice trailed away as he stared at Paddington.

" Why, Mr. Brown," he exclaimed. " You're all white! Is anything the matter? "

" Don't worry, Mr. Gruber," cried Paddington, waving his paws in the air. " It's only some of Mrs. Bird's flour. I'm afraid I can't raise my hat because it's stuck down with dumpling mixture—but I'm very glad you've come because there's something nasty in the kitchen! "

" Something nasty in the kitchen? " echoed Mr. Gruber. " What sort of thing? "

" I don't know," said Paddington, struggling with his hat. " But it's got a shadow and it's making a funny noise."

Mr. Gruber looked around nervously for something to defend himself with. " We'll soon see about that," he said, taking a warming pan off the wall.

Paddington led the way back to the kitchen and then stood to one side by the door. " After you, Mr. Gruber," he said politely.

" Er . . . thank you, Mr. Brown," said Mr. Gruber doubtfully.

He grasped the warming pan firmly in both hands and then kicked open the door. " Come out! " he cried. " Whoever you are! "

" I don't think it's a *who*, Mr. Gruber," said Paddington, peering round the door. " It's a *what*! "

" Good heavens! " exclaimed Mr. Gruber, staring

at the sight which met his eyes. "What *has* been going on?"

Over most of the kitchen there was a thin film of flour. There was flour on the table, in the sink, on the floor; in fact, over practically everything. But it wasn't the general state of the room which made Mr. Gruber cry out with surprise—it was the sight of something large and white hanging over the side of the stove.

He stared at it for a moment and then advanced cautiously across the kitchen and poked it with the handle of the warming pan. There was a loud squelching noise and Mr. Gruber jumped back as part of it broke away and fell with a plop to the floor.

"Good heavens!" he exclaimed again. "I do

believe it's some kind of dumpling, Mr. Brown. I've never seen quite such a big one before," he went on as Paddington joined him. "It's grown right out of the saucepan and pushed the lid on the floor. No wonder it made you jump."

Mr. Gruber mopped his brow and opened the window. It was very warm in the kitchen. " How ever did it get to be that size?"

" I don't really know, Mr. Gruber," said Paddington looking puzzled. " It's one of mine and it didn't start off that way. I think something must have gone wrong in the saucepan."

" I should think it has," said Mr. Gruber. " If I were you, Mr. Brown, I think I'd turn the cooker off before it catches fire and does any more damage. There's no knowing what might happen once it gets out of control.

" Perhaps, if you'll allow me," he continued tactfully, " I can give you a hand. It must be very difficult cooking for so many people."

" It is when you only have paws, Mr. Gruber," said Paddington gratefully.

Mr. Gruber sniffed. " I must say it all smells very nice. If we make some more dumplings quickly everything else should be just about ready."

As he handed Paddington the flour and suet Mr. Gruber explained how dumplings became very much larger when they were cooked and that it really needed only a small amount of mixture to make quite large ones.

"No wonder yours were so big, Mr. Brown," he said, as he lifted Paddington's old dumpling into the washing-up bowl. "You must have used almost a bag of flour."

"Two bags," said Paddington, looking over his shoulder. "I don't know what Mrs. Bird will say when she hears about it."

"Perhaps, if we buy her some more," said Mr. Gruber, as he staggered into the garden with the bowl, "she won't mind quite so much."

"That's queer," said Mr. Brown, as he stared out of the bedroom window. "There's a big white thing suddenly appeared in the garden. Just behind the nasturtiums."

"Nonsense, Henry," said Mrs. Brown. "You must be seeing things."

"I'm not," said Mr. Brown, rubbing his glasses and taking another look. "It's all white and shapeless and it looks horrible. Mr. Curry's seen it too—he's peering over the fence at it now. Do *you* know what it is, Paddington?"

"A big white thing, Mr. Brown?" repeated Paddington vaguely, joining him at the window. "Perhaps it's a snowball."

"In summer?" said Mr. Brown suspiciously.

"Henry," said Mrs. Brown. "Do come away from there and decide what you're having for lunch. Paddington's gone to a lot of trouble writing out a menu for us."

Mr. Brown took a large sheet of drawing paper from his wife and his face brightened as he studied it. It said:

MENUE
SOOP
. . .

FISH

OMMLETS

ROWST BEEF
Stew with Dumplings—Potatows—Brussle Sprowts
Pees—Cabbidge—Greyvy

. . .

MARMALADE AND CUSTERD

. . .

COFFEY

. . .

"How nice!" exclaimed Mr. Brown, when he had finished reading it. "And what a good idea putting pieces of vegetable on the side as illustrations. I've never seen that done before."

"They're not really meant to be there, Mr. Brown," said Paddington. "I'm afraid they came off my paws."

"Oh," said Mr. Brown, brushing his moustache

thoughtfully. "Mmm. Well, you know, I rather fancy some soup and fish myself."

"I'm afraid they're off," said Paddington hastily, remembering a time when he'd once been taken out to lunch and they had arrived late.

"Off?" said Mr. Brown. "But they can't be. No one's ordered anything yet."

Mrs. Brown drew him to one side. "I think we're meant to have the stew and dumplings, Henry," she whispered. "They're underlined."

"What's that, Mary?" asked Mr. Brown, who was a bit slow to grasp things at times. "Oh! Oh, I see . . . er . . . on second thoughts, Paddington, I think perhaps I'll have the stew."

"That's good," said Paddington, "because I've got it on a tray outside all ready."

"By Jove," said Mr. Brown, as Paddington staggered in breathing heavily and carrying first one plate and then another piled high with stew. "I must say I didn't expect anything like this."

"Did you cook it all by yourself, Paddington?" asked Mrs. Brown.

"Well . . . almost all," replied Paddington truthfully. "I had a bit of an accident with the dumplings and so Mr. Gruber helped me make some more."

"You're sure you have enough for your own lunch?" said Mrs. Brown anxiously.

"Oh, yes," said Paddington, trying hard not to

91

picture the kitchen, " there's enough to last for days and days."

" Well, I think you should be congratulated," said Mr. Brown. " I'm enjoying it no end. I bet there aren't many bears who can say they've cooked a meal like this. It's fit for a queen."

Paddington's eyes lit up with pleasure as he listened to Mr. and Mrs. Brown. It had been a lot of hard work but he was glad it had all been worth while— even if there was a lot of mess to clear up.

" You know, Henry," said Mrs. Brown, as Paddington hurried off downstairs to see Mr. Gruber, " we ought to think ourselves very lucky having a bear like Paddington about the house in an emergency."

Mr. Brown lay back on his pillow and surveyed the mountain of food on his plate. " Doctor MacAndrew was right about one thing," he said. " While Paddington's looking after us, whatever else happens we certainly shan't starve."

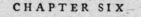

CHAPTER SIX

Trouble at the Launderette

THE GREEN front door of number thirty-two Windsor Gardens slowly opened and some whiskers and two black ears poked out through the gap. They turned first to the right, then to the left, and then suddenly disappeared from view again.

A few seconds later the quiet of the morning was broken by a strange trundling noise followed by a series of loud bumps as Paddington lowered Mr. Brown's wheelbarrow down the steps and on to the

pavement. He peered up and down the street once more and then hurried back in-doors.

Paddington made a number of journeys back and forth be-tween the house and the wheelbarrow and each time he came through the front door he was carrying a large pile of things in his paws.

There were clothes, sheets, pillow-cases, towels, several tablecloths, not to mention a number of old jerseys belonging to Mr. Curry, all of which he carefully placed in the barrow.

Paddington was pleased there was no one about. He felt sure that neither the Browns nor Mr. Curry would approve if they knew he was taking their washing to the launderette in a wheelbarrow. But an emergency had arisen and Paddington wasn't the sort of bear who allowed himself to be beaten by trifles.

Paddington had had a busy time what with one thing and another. Mrs. Bird was due back shortly before lunch and there had been a lot of clearing up to do. He had spent most of the early part of the morning going round the house with what was left of her feather duster, getting rid of flour stains from the previous day's cooking and generally making everything neat and tidy.

It was while he had been dusting the mantelpiece in the dining-room that he'd suddenly come across a small pile of money and one of Mrs. Bird's notes. Mrs. Bird often left notes about the house reminding people to do certain things. This one was headed LAUNDRY and it was heavily underlined.

Not only did it say that the Browns' laundry was due to be collected that very day, but it also had a postscript on the end saying that Mr. Curry had arranged to

send some things as well and would they please be collected.

Paddington hurried around as fast as he could but it still took him some while to gather together all the Browns' washing, and having to fetch Mr. Curry's had delayed things even more. He'd been so busy making out a list of all the things that he'd quite failed to hear the knock at the front door and had arrived there just in time to see the laundry van disappearing down the road. Paddington had run after it shouting and waving his paws but either the driver hadn't seen him, or he hadn't wanted to, for the van had turned a corner before he was even half-way down Windsor Gardens.

It was while he was sitting on the pile of washing in the hall, trying to decide what to do next and how to explain it all to Mrs. Bird, that the idea of the launderette had entered Paddington's mind.

In the past Mr. Gruber had often spoken to him on the subject of launderettes. Mr. Gruber took his own washing along to one every Wednesday evening when they stayed open late.

" And very good it is, too, Mr. Brown," he was fond of saying. " You simply put the clothes into a big machine and then sit back while it does all the work for you. You meet some interesting people as well. I've had many a nice chat. And if you don't want to chat you can always watch the washing going round and round inside the machine."

Mr. Gruber always made it sound most interesting and Paddington had often wanted to investigate the matter. The only difficulty as far as he could see was getting all the laundry there in the first place. The Browns always had a lot of washing, far too much to go into his shopping basket on wheels, and the launderette was some way away at the top of a hill.

In the end Mr. Brown's wheelbarrow had seemed the only answer to the problem. But now that he had finished loading it and was about to set off Paddington looked at it rather doubtfully. He could only just reach the handles with his paws and when he tried to lift the barrow it was much heavier than he had expected. Added to that, there was such a pile of washing on board he couldn't even see round the sides let alone over the top, which made pushing most difficult.

To be on the safe side he tied a handkerchief to the end of an old broomstick which he stuck in the front of the barrow to let people know he was coming. Paddington had often seen the same thing done on lorries when they had a heavy load, and he didn't believe in taking any chances.

Quite a number of people turned to watch Paddington's progress as he made his way slowly up the long hill. Several times he got the wheel caught in a drain and had to be helped out by a kindly passer-by, and at one point, when he had to cross a busy street, a policeman held up all the traffic for him.

Paddington thanked him very much and raised his hat to all the waiting cars and buses, which tooted their horns in reply.

It was a hot day and more than once he had to stop and mop his brow with a pillow-case, so that he wasn't at all sorry when he rounded a corner and found himself outside the launderette.

He sat down on the edge of the pavement for a few minutes in order to get his breath back and when he got up again he was surprised to find a rusty old bicycle wheel lying on top of the washing.

" I expect someone thought you were a rag-and-bone bear," said the stout, motherly lady in charge of the launderette, who came outside to see what was going on.

" A rag-and-bone bear?" exclaimed Paddington hotly. He looked most offended. " I'm not a rag-and-bone bear. I'm a laundry bear."

The lady listened while Paddington explained what he had come for and at once called out for one of the other assistants to give him a hand up the steps with his barrow.

" I suppose you're doing it for the whole street?" she asked, as she viewed the mountain of washing.

" Oh, no," said Paddington, waving his paw

vaguely in the direction of Windsor Gardens. " It's for Mrs. Bird."

" Mrs. Bird? " repeated the stout lady, looking at Mr. Curry's jerseys and some old gardening socks of Mr. Brown's which were lying on top of the pile. She opened her mouth as if she were about to say something but closed it again hurriedly when she saw Paddington staring at her.

" I'm afraid you'll need four machines for all this lot," she said briskly, as she went behind the counter. " It's a good job it's not one of our busy mornings. I'll put you in the ones at the end—eleven, twelve, thirteen and fourteen—then you'll be out of the way." She looked at Paddington. " You do know how to work them? "

" I think so," said Paddington, trying hard to remember all that Mr. Gruber had told him.

" Well, if you get into any trouble the instructions are on the wall." The lady handed Paddington eight little plastic tubs full of powder. " Here's the soap powder," she continued, " That's two tubs for each machine. You tip one tubful in a hole in the top each time a red light comes on. That'll be eleven and fourpence, please."

Paddington counted out Mrs. Bird's money and after thanking the lady began trundling his barrow along to the other end of the room.

As he steered his barrow in and out of people's

feet he looked around the launderette with interest. It was exactly as Mr. Gruber had described it to him. The washing machines, all white and gleaming, were in a line round the walls and in the middle of the room were two long rows of chairs. The machines had glass portholes in their doors and Paddington peered through several of them as he went past and watched the washing going round and round in a flurry of soapy water.

By the time he reached the end of the room he felt quite excited and he was looking forward to having a go with the Browns' washing.

Having climbed up on one of the chairs and examined the instructions on the wall, Paddington tipped his laundry out on to the floor and began sorting it into four piles, putting all Mr. Curry's jerseys into one machine and all the Browns' washing into the other three.

But although he had read the instructions most carefully Paddington soon began to wish Mr. Gruber were there to advise him. First of all there was the matter of a knob on the front of each machine. It was marked " Hot Wash " and " Warm Wash," and Paddington wasn't at all sure about it. But being a bear who believed in getting his money's worth he decided to turn them all to " Hot."

And then there was the question of the soap. Having four machines to look after made things very

difficult, especially as he had to climb up on a chair
each time in order to put it in. No sooner had a red
light gone out on one machine than another lit up
and Paddington spent the first ten minutes rushing
between the four machines pouring soap through the
holes in the top as fast as he could. There was a

nasty moment when he accidentally poured some soap
into number ten by mistake and all the water bubbled
over the side, but the lady whose machine it was was
very nice about it and explained that she'd already put
two lots in. Paddington was glad when at long last
all the red lights went out and he was able to sit back
on one of the seats and rest his paws.

He sat there for some while watching the washing

being gently tossed round and round, but it was such a nice soothing motion and he felt so tired after his labours that in no time at all he dropped off to sleep. Suddenly he was brought back to life by the sound of a commotion and by someone poking him.

It was the stout lady in charge and she was staring at one of Paddington's machines. " What have you got in number fourteen? " she demanded.

" Number fourteen? " Paddington thought for a moment and then consulted his laundry list. " I think I put some jerseys in there," he said.

The stout lady raised her hands in horror. " Oh, Else," she cried, calling to one of her assistants.

" There's a young bear here put 'is jerseys in number fourteen by mistake! "

" What! " cried Paddington. " I didn't put them in by mistake—I did it on purpose. Besides," he added, looking most worried at the expression on the lady's face, " they're not my jerseys—they're Mr. Curry's."

" Well, whoever they belong to," said the lady, as she hurriedly switched off the machine, " I hope he's long and thin."

" Oh dear," said Paddington, getting more and more worried. " I'm afraid Mr. Curry's rather short."

" That's a pity," said the lady sympathetically, " because he's got some long, thin jerseys now. You had the machine switched to ' Hot Wash ' and you should never do that with woollens. There's a special notice about that."

Paddington gazed in horror as the lady withdrew a dripping mass of wool from the machine and placed it in his barrow.

" Mr. Curry's jerseys! " he said bitterly to the world in general as he sank back in his chair.

Paddington had been a bit worried about Mr. Curry's jerseys right from the start. After the episode of the kitchen table he hadn't been very keen on meeting Mr. Curry and he'd had to lie in wait until the coast was clear before slipping into his kitchen. He'd found the jerseys in a pile by the sink but there had been nothing to say whether they were meant to be washed or not. Paddington had a nasty feeling in the back of his mind that the answer was " not," and now he was sure of it.

Paddington often found that shocks came in twos and as he sat back in his chair he received his second shock of the morning.

His eyes nearly popped out of his head as one of the other machines containing the Browns' washing began making a very strange whirring noise. The whirring was followed by several loud clicks and Paddington stared at the machine in amazement as the washing inside began to spin round faster and faster until it suddenly disappeared leaving a gaping hole in the middle.

He jumped up and peered through the porthole at the empty space where, only a few moments before, his washing had been. Then he hurriedly began to undo the knob on the side of the machine. It was all very strange and it definitely needed investigating.

Paddington wasn't quite sure what happened next, but as he opened the door a stream of hot, soapy water shot out, nearly knocking his hat off, and as he fell over backwards on to the floor most of Mrs. Bird's washing seemed to land on top of his head.

Paddington lay on his back in a pool of water and listened to the shrieks and cries going on all around

him. Then he closed his eyes, put his paws in his ears
and waited for the worst to happen.

"I think they've been having trouble up at the
launderette," said Mrs. Bird. "When I came past

in the bus just now there was quite a crowd outside and water running out of the door—not to mention bubbles everywhere."

"The launderette?" said Mrs. Brown, looking rather worried.

"That's right," said Mrs. Bird. "And Mr. Curry's had a burglary. Someone broke into his kitchen in broad daylight and took some jerseys he'd put out for mending."

Mrs. Bird had just arrived back from her holiday and she was exchanging all the news with Mrs. Brown. "If I'd known what was going on," she continued, "I wouldn't have had a minute's peace. Jonathan and Judy away and you and Mr. Brown ill in bed!" She raised her hands in horror at the thought of it all.

"We've been doing very well," said Mr. Brown, as he sat up in bed. "Paddington's been looking after us."

"Hmm," said Mrs. Bird. "That's as may be." Mrs. Bird had seen several signs of a rapid clearing up as she had made her way upstairs and she had also found the remains of her feather duster hidden in the hallstand.

"Have you seen Paddington anywhere?" asked Mrs. Brown. "He went out just now but he said he wouldn't be very long."

"No," said Mrs. Bird. "And that's another thing.

There are wheelbarrow trails right through the house. All the way up from the shed, through the kitchen and out through the front door."

"*Wheelbarrow* trails?" repeated Mr. Brown. "But we've been in bed for two days."

"That," said Mrs. Bird sternly, "is exactly what I mean!"

While the Browns were trying to solve the mystery of the wheelbarrow trails Paddington was having an even more difficult time in the launderette.

"But I only opened the door to see where the washing had gone," he explained. He was sitting on the counter wrapped in a blanket while the mess was being cleared up.

"But it hadn't gone anywhere," said the stout lady. "The things only *looked* as if they had disappeared because they were going round so fast. They always do that." She sought for words to explain what she meant. "It's a . . . it's a sort of phenomenon."

"A phen-omen-on?" repeated Paddington. "But it didn't say anything about a phenomenon in the instructions."

The lady sighed. Washing machines were rather difficult things to explain and she'd not had many dealings with bears before.

"Bubbles all over my machines!" she exclaimed.

" Water all over the floor. I've never seen such a mess! "

" Oh, dear," said Paddington sadly. " I'm in trouble again." He looked at the pile of half-washed clothes next to him. He didn't know what Mrs. Bird would say when she heard all about it, and as for Mr. Curry . . .

" I tell you what," said the stout lady as she caught sight of the expression on Paddington's face. " Seeing it's your first time here and we're not so very busy, suppose we do it all again. It would never do to have a dissatisfied customer in a launderette." She gave Paddington a wink. " Then we can put it all in the spin dryer and if I've got time I might even be able to iron it for you in the back room. After all, it's not every day we have a bear's washing to do."

Mrs. Bird surveyed the neat pile of newly-ironed laundry and then turned to Mr. and Mrs. Brown who had just come downstairs for the first time. " Well," she said approvingly, " I never expected to see this. I couldn't have done it better myself."

" I do hope it's all right, Mrs. Bird," said Paddington anxiously. " I had a bit of a phenomenon in the launderette."

" A phenomenon? " repeated Mrs. Brown. " But

you can't have a phenomenon in a washing machine."

"I did," said Paddington firmly. "And all the water came out."

"I think you must be mistaken, dear," said Mrs. Brown. "A phenomenon means something strange."

"And talking of strange things," said Mrs. Bird, looking hard at Paddington, "Mr. Curry knocked on the door a moment ago and left you a toffee. He says he's very pleased with his jerseys. He doesn't know what you've done to them but they fit him for the first time in years. They've always been too large up till now."

"Perhaps," said Mr. Brown, "there *was* a phenomenon in the washing machine after all."

Paddington felt very pleased with himself as he made his way upstairs to his room. He was glad it had turned out all right in the end. As he closed the dining-room door he just caught a remark of Mrs. Bird's.

"I think we're very lucky indeed," she said. "Looking after a big house like this for two days and doing all the washing into the bargain. That young bear's one of the old school."

Paddington puzzled over the remark for some time and in the end he went to consult his friend Mr. Gruber on the subject.

When Mr. Gruber explained to him that it meant he was very reliable, Paddington felt even more pleased. Compliments from Mrs. Bird were very rare.

"But all the better for having when they come, Mr. Brown," said Mr. Gruber. "All the better for having when they come."

CHAPTER SEVEN

Paddington Dines Out

" I vote," said Mr. Brown, " that we celebrate the occasion by visiting a restaurant. All those in favour say ' aye '."

Mr. Brown's suggestion had a mixed reception. Jonathan and Judy called out " aye " at once. Mrs. Brown looked rather doubtful and Mrs. Bird kept her eyes firmly on her knitting.

" Do you think it wise, Henry? " said Mrs. Brown. " You know what Paddington's like when we take him out. Things happen."

" It *is* his birthday," replied Mr. Brown.

"And his anniversary," said Judy. "Sort of."

The Browns were holding a council of war. It was Paddington's summer birthday. Being a bear, Paddington had two birthdays every year—one at Christmas and the other in mid-summer. That apart, he had now been with the Browns for a little over a year and it had been decided to celebrate the two occasions at the same time.

"After all, we ought to do *something*," said Mr. Brown, playing his trump card. "If we hadn't seen him that day on Paddington station we might never have met him and goodness knows where he would have ended up."

The Browns were silent for a moment as they considered the awful possibility of never having met Paddington.

"I must say," remarked Mrs. Bird, in a voice which really decided the matter, " the house wouldn't be the same without him."

" That settles it," said Mr. Brown. " I'll ring the Porchester right away and reserve a table for to-night."

" Oh, Henry," exclaimed Mrs. Brown. " Not the *Porchester*. That's such an expensive place."

Mr. Brown waved his hand in the air. " Nothing but the best is good enough for Paddington," he said generously. " We'll invite Mr. Gruber as well and make a real party of it."

" By the way," he continued, " where *is* Paddington ? I haven't seen him for ages."

" He was peering through the letter-box just now," said Mrs. Bird. " I think he was looking for the postman."

Paddington liked birthdays. He didn't get many letters—only his catalogues and an occasional postcard from his Aunt Lucy in Peru—but to-day the mantel-piece in the dining-room was already filled to over-flowing with cards and he was looking forward to some more arriving. There had been a card from each of the Browns, one from Mr. Gruber, and quite a surprising number from various people who lived in the neighbourhood. There was even an old one from Mr. Curry, which Mrs. Bird recognised as one Paddington had sent him the year before, but she had wisely decided not to point this out.

Then there were all the parcels. Paddington was

very keen on parcels—especially when they were well wrapped up with plenty of paper and string. In fact he had done extremely well for himself, and the news that they were all going out that evening as well came as a great surprise.

" Mind you," said Mrs. Brown, " you'll have to have a bath first."

" A bath!" exclaimed Paddington. " On my birthday?"

Paddington looked most upset at the thought of having a bath on his birthday.

" The Porchester is a very famous restaurant," explained Mrs. Brown. " Only the best people go there."

And, despite his protests, he was sent upstairs that afternoon with a bath cube and some soap and strict instructions not to come down again until he was clean.

Excitement in the Browns' house mounted during the afternoon and by the time Mr. Gruber arrived, looking rather self-conscious in an evening-dress suit which he hadn't worn for many years, it had reached fever pitch.

" I don't think I've ever been to the Porchester before, Mr. Brown," he whispered to Paddington in the hall. " So that makes two of us. It'll be a nice change from cocoa and buns."

Paddington became more and more excited on the journey to the restaurant. He always enjoyed seeing the lights of London and even though it was summer quite a few of them had already come on by the time they got there.

He followed Mr. Brown up the steps of the restaurant and in through some large doors, giving the man who held them open a friendly wave of his paw.

In the distance there was the sound of music and as they all gathered inside the entrance in order to leave their coats at the cloakroom, Paddington looked around with interest at the chandeliers hanging from the ceiling and at the dozens of waiters gliding to and fro.

"Here comes the head waiter," said Mr. Brown,

as a tall, superior-looking man approached. "We've booked a table near the orchestra," he called. "In the name of Brown."

The head waiter stared at Paddington. "Is the young . . . er . . . bear gentleman with you?" he asked, looking down his nose.

"With us?" said Mr. Brown. "We're with *him*. It's his party."

"Oh," said the man disapprovingly. "Then I'm afraid you can't come in."

"What!" exclaimed Paddington amid a chorus of dismay. "But I went without a second helping at lunch specially."

"I'm afraid the young gentleman isn't wearing evening dress," explained the man. "Everyone at the Porchester has to wear evening dress."

Paddington could hardly believe his ears and he gave the man a hard stare.

"Bears don't have evening dress," said Judy, squeezing his paw. "They have evening fur—and Paddington's has been washed specially."

The head waiter looked at Paddington doubtfully. Paddington had a very persistent stare when he liked, and some of the special ones his Aunt Lucy had taught him were very powerful indeed. He coughed. "I daresay," he said, "we might make an exception— just this once."

He turned and led the way through the crowded

restaurant, past tables covered with snowy white cloths and gleaming silver, towards a big round table near the orchestra. Paddington followed on close behind and by the time they reached it the man's neck had gone a funny shade of red.

When they were all seated the head waiter gave them each a huge card on which was printed a list of all the dishes. Paddington had to hold his with both paws and he stared at it in amazement.

" Well, Paddington," said Mr. Brown. " What would you like to start with? Soup? Hors d'œuvre?"

Paddington looked at his menu in disgust. He didn't think much of it at all. " I don't know what I would like, Mr. Brown," he said. " My programme's full of mistakes and I can't read it."

" *Mistakes!* " The head waiter raised one eyebrow to its full height and looked at Paddington severely. " There is never a mistake on a Porchester menu."

" Those aren't mistakes, Paddington," whispered Judy, as she looked over his shoulder. " It's French."

" French! " exclaimed Paddington. " Fancy printing a menu in French! "

Mr. Brown hastily scanned his own card. " Er . . . have you anything suitable for a young bear's treat?" he asked.

" A young bear's treat?" repeated the head waiter haughtily. " We pride ourselves that there is nothing one cannot obtain at the Porchester."

"In that case," said Paddington, looking most relieved, "I think I'll have a marmalade sandwich."

Looking around, Paddington decided a place as important as the Porchester must serve very good marmalade sandwiches, and he was anxious to test one.

"I beg your pardon, sir?" exclaimed the waiter. "Did you say a marmalade sandwich?"

"Yes, please," said Paddington. "With custard."

"For dinner?" said the man.

"Yes," said Paddington firmly. "I'm very fond of marmalade and you said there was nothing you don't have."

The man swallowed hard. In all his years at the Porchester he'd never been asked for a marmalade sandwich before, particularly by a bear. He beckoned to another waiter standing nearby. "A marmalade sandwich for the young bear gentleman," he said. "With custard."

"A marmalade sandwich for the young bear gentleman—with custard," repeated the second waiter. He disappeared through a door leading to the kitchens as if in a dream and the Browns heard the order repeated several more times before it closed. They looked around uneasily while they gave another waiter their own orders.

There seemed to be some sort of commotion going on in the kitchen. Several times they heard raised voices and once the door opened and a man in a chef's hat appeared round the corner and stared in their direction.

"Perhaps, sir," said yet another waiter, as he wheeled a huge trolley laden with dishes towards the table, "you would care for some hors d'œuvre while you wait?"

"That's a sort of salad," Mr. Brown explained to Paddington.

Paddington licked his whiskers. "It looks a very good bargain," he said, staring at all the dishes. "I think perhaps I will."

"Oh, dear," said Mrs. Brown, as Paddington began helping himself. "You're not supposed to eat it *from* the trolley, Paddington."

Paddington looked most disappointed as he watched the waiter serve the hors d'œuvre. It wasn't really quite such good value as he'd thought. But by the time the man had finished piling his plate with vegetables and pickles, salad, and a pile of interesting looking little silver onions he began to change his mind again. Perhaps, he decided, he couldn't have managed the whole trolleyful after all.

While Mr. Brown gave the rest of the orders— soup for the others followed by fish and a special omelet for Mr. Gruber—Paddington sat back and prepared to enjoy himself.

"Would you like anything to drink, Paddington?" asked Mr. Brown.

" No, thank you, Mr. Brown," said Paddington. " I have a bowl of water."

" I don't think that's drinking water, Mr. Brown," said Mr. Gruber tactfully. " That's to dip your paws in when they get sticky. That's what's known as a paw bowl."

" A paw bowl? " exclaimed Paddington. " But I had a bath this afternoon."

" Never mind," said Mr. Brown hastily. " I'll send for the lemonade waiter—then you can have an orange squash or something."

Paddington was getting more and more confused. It was all most complicated and he'd never seen so many waiters before. He decided to concentrate on eating for a bit.

" Most enjoyable," said Mr. Gruber a few minutes later when he had finished his soup. " I shall look forward to my omelet now." He looked across the table at Paddington. " Are you enjoying your hors d'œuvre, Mr. Brown? "

" It's very nice, Mr. Gruber," said Paddington, staring down at his plate with a puzzled expression on his face. " But I think I've lost one of my onions."

" You've what? " asked Mr. Brown. It was difficult to hear what Paddington was saying for the noise the orchestra was making. It had been playing quite sweetly up until a moment ago but suddenly it had started making a dreadful row. It was something

to do with one of the saxophone players in the front
row. He kept shaking his instrument and then trying
to blow it, and all the while the conductor was glaring
at him.

" My onion! " exclaimed Paddington. " I had six
just now and when I put my fork on one of them it
suddenly disappeared. Now I've only got five."

Mrs. Brown began to look more and more
embarrassed as Paddington got down off his seat and
began peering under the tables. " I do hope he finds
it soon," she said. Everyone in the restaurant seemed
to be looking in their direction and if they weren't
actually pointing she knew they were talking about
them.

" Gosh! " exclaimed Jonathan suddenly. He pointed towards the orchestra. " There *is* Paddington's onion! "

The Browns turned and looked at the orchestra. The saxophone player seemed to be having an argument with the conductor.

" How can I be expected to play properly," he said bitterly, " when I've got an onion in my instrument? And I've a good idea where it came from too! "

The conductor followed his gaze towards the Browns, who hurriedly looked the other way.

" For heaven's sake don't tell Paddington," said Mrs. Brown. " He'll only want it back."

" Never mind," said Mr. Gruber, as the door leading to the kitchen opened. " I think my omelet's just coming."

The Browns watched as a waiter entered bearing a silver dish which he placed on a small spirit stove near their table. Mr. Gruber had ordered an omelet " flambée ", which meant it was set on fire just before it was served. " I don't know when I had one of those last," he said. " I'm looking forward to it."

" I must say it looks very nice," said Mr. Brown, twirling his moustache thoughtfully. " I rather wish I'd ordered one myself now."

" Come along, Paddington," he called, as the waiter

set light to the pan. " Come and see Mr. Gruber's omelet. It's on fire."

" What! " cried Paddington, poking his head out from beneath the table. " Mr. Gruber's omelet's on fire? "

He stared in astonishment at the waiter as he bore the silver tray with its flaming omelet towards the table.

" It's all right, Mr. Gruber," he called, waving his paws in the air. " I'm coming! "

Before the Browns could stop him, Paddington had grabbed his paw bowl and had thrown the contents over the tray. There was a loud hissing noise and before the astonished gaze of the waiter Mr. Gruber's omelet slowly collapsed into a soggy mess in the bottom of the dish.

Several people near the Browns applauded. " What an unusual idea," said one of them. " Having the cabaret act sit at one of the tables just like anyone else."

One old gentleman in particular who was sitting by himself at the next table laughed no end. He had been watching Paddington intently for some time and now he began slapping his knee at each new happening.

" Crikey! " said Jonathan. " We're for it now." He pointed towards a party of very important-looking people, led by the head waiter, who were approaching the Browns' table.

They stopped a few feet away and the head waiter pointed at Paddington. " That's the one," he said. " The one with the whiskers! "

The most important-looking man stepped forward. " I'm the manager," he announced. " And I'm afraid I must ask you to leave. Throwing water over a waiter. Putting onions in a saxophone. Ordering marmalade sandwiches. You'll get the Porchester a bad name."

Mr. and Mrs. Brown exchanged glances. " I've never heard of such a thing," said Mrs. Bird. " If that bear goes we all go."

" Hear! Hear! " echoed Mr. Gruber.

" And if you go I shall go too," came a loud voice from the next table.

Everyone looked round as the old gentleman who had been watching the proceedings rose and waved a finger at the manager. " May I ask why this young bear's being asked to leave? " he boomed.

The manager began to look even more worried, for the old gentleman was one of his best customers and he didn't want to offend him. " It annoys the other diners," he said.

" Nonsense! " boomed the old gentleman. " I'm one of the other diners and I'm not annoyed. Best thing that's happened in years. Don't know when I've enjoyed myself so much." He looked down at Paddington. " I should like to shake you by the paw, bear. It's about time this place was livened up a bit."

" Thank you very much," said Paddington, holding out his paw. He was a bit overawed by the old gentleman and he wasn't at all sure what it was all about anyway.

The old gentleman waved the waiters and the manager to one side and then turned to Mr. Brown. " I'd better introduce myself," he said. " I'm Sir Huntley Martin the marmalade king."

" I've been in marmalade for fifty years," he boomed, " and been comin' here for thirty. Never heard anyone ask for a marmalade sandwich before. Does me old heart good."

Paddington looked most impressed. " Fancy being in marmalade for fifty years! " he exclaimed.

" I hope you'll allow me to join you," said Sir Huntley. " I've done a good many things in my life but I don't think I've ever been to a bear's birthday party before."

The old gentleman's presence seemed to have a magical effect on the manager of the Porchester, for he had a hurried conference with the head waiter and in no time at all a procession started from the kitchen headed by a waiter bearing a silver tray on which was another omelet for Mr. Gruber.

Even the head waiter allowed himself a smile and he gave Paddington a special autographed menu to take away as a souvenir and promised that in future there would always be a special section for marmalade sandwiches.

It was a hilarious party of Browns who finally got up to go. Paddington was so full of good things he had a job to get up at all. He had a last lingering look at the remains of an ice-cream on his plate but decided that enough was as good as a feast. He'd enjoyed himself no end and after a great deal of thought he left a penny under his plate for the waiter.

Sir Huntley Martin seemed very sad that it had all come to an end. " Most enjoyable," he kept booming as they left the table. " Most enjoyable. Perhaps," he added hopefully to Paddington, " you'll do me the honour of visiting my factory one of these days."

" Oh, yes, please," said Paddington. " I should like that very much."

As they left the restaurant he waved good-bye with his paw to all the other diners, several of whom applauded when the orchestra struck up " Happy Birthday to You."

Only Mrs. Bird seemed less surprised than the others, for she had seen Sir Huntley slip something in the conductor's hand.

It had become really dark outside while they had been eating their dinner and all the lights in the street were on. After they had said good-bye to Sir Huntley, and because it was a special occasion, Mr. Brown

drove round Piccadilly
Circus so that Padding-
ton could see all the
coloured signs work-
ing.

Paddington peered
out of the car window
and his eyes grew larger
and larger at the sight
of all the red, green
and blue lights flash-
ing on and off and
making patterns in the
sky.

"Have you enjoyed
yourself, Paddington?"
asked Mr. Brown as they went round for the second
time.

"Yes, thank you very much, Mr. Brown," exclaimed
Paddington.

Altogether Paddington thought it had been a
wonderful day and he was looking forward to writing
a letter to his Aunt Lucy telling her everything about it.

After giving a final wave of his paw to some
passers-by, he raised his hat to a policeman who
signalled them on, and then settled back in his seat
to enjoy the journey home with Mr. Gruber and the
Browns.

"I think," he announced sleepily, as he gave one final stare at the fast-disappearing lights, "I would like to have an anniversary every year!"

"And so say all of us, Mr. Brown," echoed Mr. Gruber from the back of the car. "And so say all of us!"